Nick Maes lives in London, where he has worked – among other things – in theatre, fashion, radio, and as a journalist. This is his first novel.

Praise for *Not Dark Yet*:

'Naive . . . is the reader who ignores the quieter contributions of writers like Nick Maes, a debut novelist whose book . . . provides a new insight into the problem of how to deal with a human heart in a man's body' *The Times*

'This is a comedy about the gulf between the old and the young – a gulf that can be bridged, but only with willing compromise on both sides. When two inflated egos exist side by side, sparks will inevitably fly. Light, humane and amusing' *Gay Times*

'A wonderful, haunting book. Run out and buy it' *The Scene*

'A tender yet funny account of the making of a genuine love story' *Glasgow Evening Times*

'A funny, touching love story, between a most unlikely pair, this debut novel promises great things' *Birmingham Post*

NOT DARK YET

Nick Maes

review

First published in Great Britain in 2002
by REVIEW

An imprint of Headline Book Publishing

First published in paperback in 2003

10 9 8 7 6 5 4 3 2 1

ISBN 0 7553 0012 2

Typeset in Garamond Light by
Palimpsest Book Production Limited,
Polmont, Stirlingshire

Printed and bound in Great Britain by
Mackays of Chatham plc, Chatham, Kent

Headline Book Publishing
A division of Hodder Headline
338 Euston Road
London NW1 3BH

www.reviewbooks.co.uk
www.hodderheadline.com

For:

My mother, father and my sisters

Ellis Flyte

Kate Jones

Mary Pachnos

Jake Paltenghi

Many thanks to Geraldine Cooke, Janice Brent, Bob McDevitt, David Grogan and Hazel Orme for their help; and to Angela Billows, Iddi Abeidi Iddi, Nad and a raft of others who have all been tremendously supportive.

ME

My Filofax is well knackered. Look at it: bloated with paper, the leather's scuffed and stained and its tatty guts are held in place with a rubber band. Filofax. Filofux more like it. *Filus fuxialus. Filosia fuxalii.* If I'm not mistaken, the etymology of Filofax is Latin. The word *filo* means friend, from the phrase *filosianus alotus*, or pastry for many mates, and the word *fux*, I believe, is self-explanatory. That's how my organiser is divided at any rate. It's instantly apparent who is a friend and who is . . . not. The friends remain steadfastly in place and the *fux*, inevitably, end up Biroed out. Looking now at the scrawled-through names and numbers it appears there have been quite a few of the latter. It's surprising how one forgets them so quickly.

Let's start with the friends. According to my crumpled and greasy A–Z insert I have 573 entries that are all filed under the friends, or *filo*, section. If I'm honest, I'm just the teensiest bit anal about this insert; the diary bit can go to hell – it's the names and numbers that get me. Someone once suggested I cross-reference it all, so apart from an alphabetical list I could have groupings by profession, age, specialist interests, etc. I was momentarily taken by the idea until they added star signs, food preferences and hair colouring. I felt like a prick. Anyway, 571 of these entries are technically acquaintances, people I like and get on with; some I see quite a lot, but they're not *real* friends. They are some of the dozens I know from the party scene, but they are not the people I'd call if I needed to.

That leaves me with two best friends. Well, one, actually, Erin, because the other is Mum and she doesn't strictly count as a friend. Er-in, probably of Nordic origin. *Er* is an archaic word for a small loaf of bread and *in* is an equally obscure name for an object you put in a bucket. Er-in: roll-mop. Herring. Erin. Bollocks.

I've known Erin for six years, ever since my move to London in '83. We met through a mutual mate, found ourselves sharing a flat together and immediately became best pals. She's the person I call first, no matter what, like her with me. It's been like that ever since we became completely enmeshed with each other one shitty Sunday afternoon at an amusement arcade on the Strand.

'Jake, can you skive off work tomorrow?'

'Yeah, s'pose so. Why?'

'I'm going to have an abortion. I need a mate with me.'

I was playing Lucky Sevens at the time. I didn't win, though.

Early next morning the two of us went off to a surgery in Clapham, as recommended by the Marie Stopes advice people. It was not a nice place. It looked grim from the outside but, then, how should an abortion clinic look? The building was in a street off the common, a red-brick Victorian villa that, years ago, had been painted white. The receptionist showed us into a large room furnished with old dining chairs that lined the walls. I looked around at the other women and felt surprised: I'd expected to see a room full of Erins, blonde skinny girls who had all made cock-ups. But she was the only one who fitted that bill, every other type of woman was there. They were sixteen to forty-something, some with husbands, boyfriends, some by themselves and one with me. The waiting room was grubby; it looked like a provincial dentist's. On a table was a stack of magazines, mainly the *Lady* and *Country Life*.

'Have you seen this, babes?'

Erin didn't reply. Instead she sucked at her bottom lip and made as if she were about to sit her O levels. She looked young, vulnerable and panic-stricken.

'What a fab place. "Situated by its own lake in grounds stretching to 14.5 acres . . . Elizabethan manor house with three reception rooms and eight bedrooms." We could set up a B and B with an additional trout-farm facility.'

Erin took my hand and held on tight; she'd never done that before.

'Oh, my God. What about a Georgian mansion with its very own recording studio and adjacent stud farm? Perfect for a Catherine the Great routine with the Bros boys.'

Erin had gone pale and was staring at an invisible spot somewhere in the middle of the room. No one was actually talking; there was the occasional murmur, though.

'How about an island just off St Lucia? Just two point five million dollars with its own air-strip.'

'Jake, for God's sake, cut the fantasy bollocks. Sod *Country Life*.'

I wasn't mucking with Erin while awaiting termination – I loved her, she was my best friend; all I wanted to do was distract her. Yes, it was fantasy nonsense, but then that's me, that's why we got on so well. She was taken off to dress up in a gown while I sat and waited. I thumbed through the *Lady*. It seemed incongruous that an abortion clinic should supply a magazine that was half full of adverts for nannies.

It felt like a week passed before I was allowed upstairs to find a deathly pale girl dwarfed by a monumental bed. 'How you feeling, baby?'

'Get me out of here, Jake, I need a drink.'

'You sure?'

'Please, Jake, c'mon. I want out of here now. Let's go. I want to sit under a duvet snuggled up to you. I need a vodka and I don't want to think.'

Our main drinking hole then was a wine bar called Solange's. Just off Leicester Square, it was tucked down one of the alleys that skirt around the theatres on the east side of the Charing Cross Road. We didn't go into the West End after her abortion (we went home then and laid waste to a bottle of vodders) but a couple of days later we were back there. The idea was to have a swift drink then bugger off in our respective directions. A hasty drink with Erin invariably failed: we got bollocksed on three bottles of Beaujolais Nouveau.

'Jakey, what's the longest you've ever had a relationship for?'

I had to think carefully. 'About three days, I'd imagine.'

'Don't you ever want something that's more permanent, more long-term?'

That was six years ago, I was eighteen years old, and not even remotely thinking of settling down with a life partner. 'Babes, I've got you. You're the one I'm with. You know why? Because sex is never going to cloud up our friendship.'

I was right, sex didn't. Not between her and me or between our respective partners and us. Not even when Erin found herself such a serious boyfriend that she settled down and got married, for God's sake. She and Dave had a great wedding: there were just four of us (Dave's best man making up the numbers) at a Las Vegas matrimonial drive-thru. It's a pity that city doesn't do equally consumerist divorces 'cos then we could all have returned last year for their neon annulment. Erin and I don't share a place together now, but we still see as much of each other as we always have. And I still don't have a serious suitor, which brings me neatly to the *fux*.

I've had a variety of boyfriends. That sounds too chocolate box, way too pick 'n' mix. I've had a steam-room full of boyfriends (more realistic, perhaps, since it seems to me that every liaison I've ever had started with a frantic wank in some sauna or other). It has to be said that an assignation in a straight sauna is a bit of a thrill. A weekday daytime, and I'm wrapped up in a slightly grotty civic-centre towel staring into space and making no effort at communicating with the two guys who sit one each side of me. It is very quiet, the pine sauna cabin has had no maintenance for years so one bench is very wobbly and the wood above the coals has been charred black. Smells a bit too – sweaty feet and old vests.

I glance to the left and do a minuscule double-take. The guy is a tiny, skinny Mediterranean type and it looks like he's stuffed a prize-winning marrow under his towel. I itch at my balls and pull at my cock through the scuzzy flannelling wrapped around my waist – all a bit nonchalant, slightly testosteroney, a man kinda thing to do in the sauna. I suppose it's some sort of primal rutting complex; everybody does it with just the right look of self-satisfaction coupled with relief beamed at the ceiling.

But when you have a grope and a stretch and quickly catch another's eye something else altogether kicks in. The opening salvo, and you wait for just the tiniest flicker of recognition. You've gotta be careful, the bloke you're interested in may very well be the genuine gym bunny, the definite article, a bit Dagenham and very unfriendly – the type of diamond geezer 'oo 'ates poofs. Not that Marrow Man fits the bill, far too quirky hairdresser. Marrow Man looks back – ***rule one***: when cruising in a sauna never ever look friendly. Smiling is *de trop*; a slightly anguished expression with just a hint of frown does nicely. Marrow Man's tiny face is crowned by two startlingly large caterpillar eyebrows, which have knitted themselves into the requisite grimace. It's working. We both look like we're struggling with our inner demons (which is bollocks, of course, there's nothing inner or demon about it, it's just the look you need to have). ***Rule two***: don't stare straight away, just the occasional glance (once every fifteen seconds should do the trick). The other man leaves the cabin. This is where eye-contact oscillates between pained expression and groin. Your personal gropes can now happen at more regular intervals, or for the seasoned swordsman nudging your towel up and down with your hard-on can be played to great effect. ***Rule three***: after successfully completing the above two steps you can now stare full on and begin to unfold your towel, remembering to look serious still. Marrow Man pulls back his towel and I fuck up on the looking-serious bit. Strike marrow, add torpedo. How this boy manages to stay conscious with an erection like that defies belief. How this scrawny little guy can have a cock that size is beyond comprehension. Maybe that's why he's so skinny – anything he eats goes straight to nurturing his titanic knob rather than feeding any other part of his body. My nonchalant, frowny expression falters, it's more eyes-out-on-stalks (think Tom and Jerry on mescaline or Scooby-Doo on dope). Well, no time like the present – you never know if anyone is going to walk in on you. Time for a wank. Wow. Fab.

Torpedo was Mediterranean, Italian and not a hairdresser: he worked at the sauna. I'm not wholly sure of what a sauna operative does – changes the odd towel and patrols the cabins, I guess. Jerking off with customers must be an extra-curricular activity. Communicating with tricks is also kind of additional to the job in hand. Normally after that first burst of furtive penile gymnastics a quick knowing smile (now allowed), followed by a hasty retreat to the showers (to clean up), is the order of the day. Actually, talking with someone is a bit of a novelty – it destroys the anonymous fantasy and, let's get real, implies there may be something more than mutual self-abuse. I guess you've got to be pretty desperate to prolong a five-minute toss into something more social. It's akin to farting loudly at a cocktail party and hoping that your appalled neighbour might stay on and chat happily about the latest movie release. So, cut to the chase, Torpedo is Giovanni, I am most definitely desperate. And here's me now making social niceties after carnal severities in a tacky Camden Town sauna. But, hey, we're chatting. Maybe Gio's as needy as I am. Time for top-spin.

'Yeah, I'm a designer. Costume jewellery, accessories. It's a bijou design-led line.'

'Really?'

'Yes. I've just finished a collection for my company, cutting-edge stuff, very now.'

What am I on? Very now? I'm sorry, ***reality check one***: designer, well, yes if you count faffing around with beads and a few sequins, ear-wires and a glue-gun. Accessories? I make belts – there's only so much a strap of leather can do around your waist. Cutting-edge bijou bollocks. My company? As if. But it sounds good. I'm a designer, wow, even beginning to believe that line myself.

My fashion affirmations were working. The more they were repeated the more real they became. Paris, London, Bergdorf's, Barney's. New York City, New York City. Hell, it was a mantra.

'Yeah, we've just finished showing in New York, London's this week.'

Gio looks impressed – spot on.

'You have to go to New York?'

'Yes, it's one of those mixed blessings, you know?' Like I do – I don't think.

'Travelling is fun and all that, but it's hard work at the end of the day. Chatting to buyers, having to be sociable, it's knackering. All most people see are the party invites and the whole *glamorousness* of it all. But I can tell you, chatting to pterodactyls from Barney's and big-hair scary drag from Bergdorf's really is shite.'

My world-weary fashioned-out speech was working perfectly. I was a hard-done-by fashionista with an exhausting international life spent reeling from one fashion capital to the next. I was the type of trendy bitch who was in season six months before anyone else. ***Reality check two***: New York, Bergdorf's and Barney's were total fabrication, especially as the Big Apple was not for another week. But what the heck?

'What parties?'

Now we were on a subject I could really excel at. Even though my professional existence had been spuriously elevated to that of silver-haired-chubby-orange-skinned-villa-rich-Milanese-faggot-design supremo, my party credentials were genuinely second to none. For some reason (better known to half a dozen PRs rather than to me) I was on every list going. If not forthcoming, party invites were always got. I could get in anywhere and was made honorary member of any number of clubs. How's this for bullshit? Having upset Bonnie Marcinello by not returning her calls I knew that getting VIP passes to George Michael's party would be hard. I tried the record label.

'Yeah, love you to be there, Jake, get tickets from Bonnie.'

Bugger, but that wasn't going to scupper my chances. One fake American accent and a call to Bonnie's office on the day of the party: 'Yeah, hi, Marcus Quark from *Variedy*. I'd like a couple of invites for George's pardy.'

'Marcus . . .'

'Quark, *Variedy*.'

'No problem, can you send a bike?'

Mission completed, easy. Much vodka and two Es later, enter one deranged ligger with his best mate Erin to George's mega Westway thrash. Q one v. pissed-off publicity person: 'Who gave you tickets, Jakey?'

With bad accent: 'Ever heard of Marcus Quark?'

Parties and invites were never a problem. Gio wanted in and, it has to be said, there ain't no way I was going to keep him out. Nosiree, novelty-caterpillar-torpedo man could definitely join in and, yes, there was a party tonight.

'What time do you finish?'

'Six o'clock.'

'Great, I'll call you at eight with the details.'

Shower and gone.

THEM

Home is a shared flat on the third floor of a deco block that still has an almost full complement of its original tenants. Chiltern Mansions is situated on the unfashionable side of Hampstead. No, I'd never realised there was such a place but, believe you me, Gospel Oak is it. The apartment is cheap; it overlooks Parliament Hill and is like living on a liner in a time-warp because the hallways are full of railings and portholes and the metalwork is picked out in a cheery blue. The area's seriously out of kilter with the rest of London. It supports the kind of corner shops that would better suit a rural community *circa* 1950 rather than a down-at-heel late eighties inner-city borough. In my local store there always seem to be a preponderance of Battenbergs and fairies, hammy smells and doilies as well as my veteran neighbours: an ageing populace of old socialists, ancient seamen and blue-rinses. A useful tip: if you end up in a block full of the genteel and elderly try to get the ones who are hard of hearing or absent-minded in the flat next door to yours. That's what we have, the perfect neighbours who either can't hear the noise racketing out from the ghetto-blaster, or have forgotten why it has annoyed them in the first place.

Our flat is full of stuff: poncy Moroccan inlaid tables, massive sofas suffocating under dozens of animal-skin cushions, and plants of every description. There's a piano that has never been played, paintings and wood blocks fill every conceivable space on the walls, along with mirrors, postcards and all the collected shit of two fanatic hoarders. The floors are covered in several layers of underfelt, pre-Festival-of-Britain carpet and an enormous array of mats and rugs; it is dusty, Freudian, boho chic realised as only a couple of artsy fags can muster. So, the flatmate is Patrick, a landscape gardener, a bit grand and spectacularly camp. He is the only guy I've ever met who needed a butt plug for his vowels.

There was mail: the bank, loan people and Barclaycard – I was feeling distinctly unloved – and there were messages on the answerphone:

'Jake, why weren't you in work today? Call me.' Beep.

'Jake, it's Max here. Louis's died and I've decided everyone should meet at your place to discuss the issue; I'm too busy to do it alone. We'll all be round at eight, no need to cook or anything, sorry it's short notice.' Beep.

Dead? Frig. Death seemed pretty radical. I couldn't quite get my head around Louis snuffing it. He'd not seemed that terminal when I last saw him. I was incredulous; people don't just die, do they? I didn't really believe it. It was a sick joke. Bloody Max, the precious little antique-dealer creep, had decided on my behalf to hold an inquest in my gaff. And what was doubly irksome was the fact that (a) I hadn't counted on Louis needing a meeting, and (b) I'd got my hot date with Gio lined up for the same time. Even I knew which had to take precedence. The hot date would have to wait, and I would have to clear up the flat and concentrate on the dead Louis. I'd also have to call work – handy that I had the Louis excuse. I started with four days' worth of dirty plates, progressed to an annual communing with the vacuum cleaner in the sitting room by way of the off-licence (there might not be any food but booze was a necessity) via a phone call with work: 'Hi, Richard, Jake . . . Yeah, sorry I wasn't in . . . An old friend has died . . . Yeah, very unexpected, it's knocked us all for six . . . Yeah, I'll be in tomorrow . . . Thanks for understanding . . . Okay, then. 'Bye.'

It's amazing what a self-righteous tone coupled with news of death can achieve, in this particular case *carte blanche* to skive off work for a wank. Well, if folks were coming round to deal with Louis, I had to get my homework done and contact his rabbi. Louis, bless, must be the only closet-queen Jew who, at death's door, decides to engage the services of a radical lesbian rabbi. Gordy Goldstein was something else.

'I am sorry to hear the sad news. What I suggest is that we celebrate Louis's sexuality. We should enjoy his very gayness.'

God – or should that be Yahweh? – only knows why, because Louis in all his forty-odd years never had: the poor bugger spent his entire life denying being gay to his ancient parents and moaning about never getting shagged to the brotherhood. Nope, I didn't think a celebration of his sexuality was a very good idea.

'Perhaps we could have a *shiva* for his sexuality.'

'Perhaps we should forget his sexuality altogether. Can't you imagine the state his old parents are going to be in? "First we lose a son, but oy veh!, now we've gained a faggot."' I didn't think the planned luridly pansified semi-kosher version of Louis's patchy sex life was going to work. Not for him or for his mum and dad.

But Gordy wasn't going to give up that easily – she'd got an agenda and that included sex. It was becoming more and more apparent that this eulogy was more about militant-Goldstein-dyke-you-likedom than anything Louis would want. I suggested we sat on it and talked the next day. I'd got Max and pals to prepare for.

Patrick – the flatmate – was, thankfully, off on some job ('It really is the most *wooon*derful garden, positively sweeping, darling, it just rears up at you, like a, like the most *faaa*bulous seascape . . .'). Max (the gilt-edged curio queen), Pedro (Max's even more precious lispy Spanish boyfriend), Villy (Pedro's priceless bulldog) and the other assorted fashiony faggoty types who were headed towards my place were destined never to bond with Patrick. They just weren't each other.

I sat down in the living room by myself. It was strange to see it looking tidy. Everything was strange, especially Louis not being around any more. The reality started to kick in. He was gone; I felt unnerved, a little bit sick. He'd snuffed it when I was in the sauna, probably at just the time I met Gio. The phone rang.

'Hi, darling, it's me.'

'Hello?'

'Jake, it's me, Erin.'

I was feeling chewed up. I didn't normally feel like that, I was too tough, too Jake-the-lad. But this wasn't normal.

'Jake? What's wrong?'

'Louis's dead.'

This was it, I'd said it, the-Louis's-dead thing; I was going to blub. I could feel the tears squirt into my eyes, my voice desperately trying to cover it up. 'I've just got a message from Max . . .' My hand and the receiver were wet, so was my cheek – the voice was still bearing up though. '. . . and he said that Louis died today.' My voice had gone. I was whispering and snivelling. 'I don't know what to do.'

There was quiet at the other end. Not an embarrassed silence, it was simply enough hush to allow me to cry.

'What the fuck? I don't friggin' cry.'

'It doesn't matter, Jake.'

'I don't fucking cry. Fucking Louis. He's actually gone and fucking done it.' I was sobbing gaspy-snotty-red-eyed-men-don't-cry tears. It was the type of bawling that empties your insides.

'What do you mean, "done it"? He hardly topped himself, Jake. Look, I think I should come over.'

'You don't need to, I'll be fine.'

'You're not.'

'I am. I only wanted to let you know, that's all. I mean, I knew he was going to die and all that, I just never believed he would. And now he has. I don't think I've ever felt like this. I don't know how to feel.'

'I'm coming over. I'll get a cab, I'll be with you in fifteen minutes.'

Erin arrived to find me wrapped up in a huge turd-coloured

Arab coat – my comfort blanket. Eyes red, cheeks stinging. We sat together on the dusty sofa with a bottle of vodders. I was making super-human efforts to contain my tears: it didn't work, I was crying again.

'Jake, it's fine to cry, he was your friend, you asshole.'

'It's just that everything feels so lonely. I mean, Louis's gone. I feel abandoned.'

Erin put her arms around me. Life had always seemed so permanent, it was for ever, and to my mind Louis's illness had been no different. It had looked set to rattle on into eternity inside him and he, in turn, would remain indefinitely sick.

'You know, I think he died at the time I was cruising the boy I picked up in the sauna.'

'Jake, I don't need the details. Now, who did you say was heading over this evening?'

Erin, like Patrick, was no fan of the queeny little party who were about to descend upon my flat. She found the idea of them being keen to sort out 'the Louis issue' particularly distasteful. 'Christ, Jake, Louis was a friend to you lot – at least, he was to you. Do you think he's a problem – an *issue* – to sort out?'

'I was only telling you what Max said. He was never an issue with me.'

I'd first met Louis three years ago: we picked each other up after an Imagination concert. Louis was really into campy disco – Imagination, for those of you who don't know, don't come much camper – he loved it. I still do, I adore a bit of funky handbag over trance any day. Pick-up is probably overstating it a bit, though; we were never going to be bed buddies. The one occasion we actually got into the sack together was an unmitigated disaster. It wasn't a tissue issue and our association was all the better for that; it meant we could stay friends. And we did. It was Louis who first suggested I go blond.

'Yup, blond, know what I mean, Jake?'

'You really think so, Lou?'

'Yup, very Roman, know what I mean? Let me book you tomorrow.'

I was pulled on to his barber's chair and into his inner sanctum, a hard core of about a dozen whom Louis regarded as the cream of his crop. Louis, you should know, knew hundreds of people – even more than I did. He'd spend hours each day cultivating them, calling for a quick chat between blow-dries, gossiping, trying to fix up drinks parties. Wholesale introduction was his mission. He thought of himself as the doyen of some sophisticated (rather than hairdressing) salon and defined himself by his super-extended fraternity. Being part of his intimate circle was an honour. He was hilarious, party to all the gossip around town, best friends with all the PRs going (he knew a lot of Z-list celebs) and was a font of extremely good information when it came to what was happening on the party circuit. In retrospect it was Louis who got me on to all those fabulous guest lists. Good on him. It was through Louis that I added at least another five dozen names to my Filofax – every last one of them in the *filo* department – and it was some of them who were now headed towards my place.

Gabby, the deceased's sculptress pal, arrived first. It seemed to me that no matter what she spent on her appearance she still looked like a ball of lard rolled in dog hair. Max adored her. Why Gabby had such a steely grip over someone who was even more impeded by the veneer of beauty than myself (i.e. Max) was a complete mystery. What was it that captivated him? Perhaps it was her patina. Then the great Max and Pedro swept into the flat just as I imagined a stereophonic Princess Margaret might, had she been co-joined at the hip with her Siamese other half – disdainful, dainty and dog-ridden. It didn't look good. It seemed a pretty heavy indictment on the freshly dead Louis that the best he could hope for in the despatch-committee stakes was us. But, then, the only reason that this weird assortment of queens and fag-hag was gathered together was because we were his friends.

Pedro started: 'I've been looking for coffins, darlings, and found this super undertaker's in Fulham called Bodies in Heaven or something. They're *totally* gay, you know, vewy chic, vewy handy, and they have the most wonderful selection of caskets and the like.'

I think Pedro's enthusiasm for gay gravediggers surprised everyone, including Villy.

'Now, there's this gorgeous coffin in black lacquer that has these lovely little gold flowers stencilled in swags awound the lid. Louis would die for it.'

I believe the designer funeral was born at that moment. It was the type of idea *The Clothes Show* could run with. It was a fantastic opportunity to consider the finer issues of whether peasant pyres were in or not. Jeff Banks might think it time for you to take your extinguished loved one to Varanasi, wrap them up in tweed and burn them on a *ghat* on the Ganges. Or perhaps a more current interment would fit the bill: Karen Franklin, always cutting edge, would definitely go for a space burial. Think interesting fabrics again, Gore-Tex or Microfibre: durability is the key here, especially if the cherished cadaver is going to bounce around for eternity in a void. You'd really want them looking good for ever, surely? Erin was glaring at me. I had glazed over and fallen into a TV-fantasy-land delirium. I could imagine what another three hours on what to stick the stiff in would be like. I was finding it difficult to keep up with the drivel.

'Enough,' I said. 'Don't you think a pine box would do the trick – an orange crate, even?'

There was silence.

'Ahhh, I see, vewy clever . . . You're thinking Shaker, aren't you? I think that might be extwemely effective. Or what about those amazing people in the States? You know, the ones who live like it was two hundred years ago. The Hamish, I think. They're Dutch or something. Or Scottish. I bet they do darling coffins.' Pedro had brought everything back to the rarefied world of Conran cremations.

Gabby was not to be left out. 'Louis was always so with it. Couldn't we think along more modern lines and make some sort of art piece to bury him in?'

It was too much. I couldn't bear another word. 'Gabby, Louis was a hairdresser, not a fucking pharaoh.'

'The issue' was speeded up. Headstones and sculpture were discussed, readings decided upon and a group decision was taken that Louis wouldn't be outed to his parents on his big day. An uneasy truce about the coffin was reached – dictated primarily by budget. It was now nearly midnight; we'd (or, more like, I'd) got through a few bottles of white as well as the vodders with Erin. It was time for everyone to sod off home. Damn, I'd not called Gio, I'd just have to do it tomorrow. I needed everyone out of the flat – I'd done enough funereal stuff and it was time to party. I fancied hitting town and getting laid. Erin was gasping for civilisation too.

LOWLIFE

'Gio? Hi, it's Jake. We met at the sauna yesterday.'

'Hi. What happen to you yesterday?'

'I'm sorry I got caught up, I'll tell you about it later. I've got tickets for the Westwood and Hamnett parties tonight if you're interested . . . D'you want to eat first?'

For someone so friggin' broke, the amount of money I spent on restaurants was pretty damn amazing. We're not talking Stockpots or Centrales here, but Signor Zilli's and Jules' Bar in Jermyn Street. What couldn't I spend in a restaurant? We decided on Jules' Bar.

'Can you be there in an hour?'

It was never an obvious spot for a fashion queen. Actually it was altogether a bit Alice-band and Darius, but fun all the same. It was New Yorky and expensive, with seats that stretched around the central bar for surf 'n' turf, oysters and champagne. The bar staff were fantastic plus-arama. The guys never forgot my name and always made just the right fuss. It was very reassuring, especially for someone with an over-inflated ego. I should also admit to being the only customer who ever wore a blue sequin jacket with same blue silk/satin boxer shorts – *quel* peroxide-disco-diva-on-acid –

so perhaps the extraordinary recall of the bodega boys wasn't that marvellous. The guys at Jules' loved me, sequins and all.

I got there at eight and Gio followed twenty minutes later. I went for it, desperate to impress. We had champagne. Still living my multimillionaire fantasy, I ordered oysters, which neither of us ate. We got quite high on the booze. The City types brayed, but none as loudly as me regaling the new date with my own exploits, piss elegance and self-aggrandisement. We took an E each and came up while we sat at the bar. Gio, I have to say, was a bit of a catch. Dead sexy in a squirty-quirky way and funny too. His English was creative, even more so after a tab.

'Which cunty you born in?'

It only took one missing vowel to have me giggling mindlessly into the champagne. I was reeling a little and feeling as horny as hell. I love that first rush of E. It starts as a tingle in your toes and then, *boom*: it sprints up your body. It's the warmest chemical buzz you'll ever have. My eyesight began to flicker and my head to spin as the drug took hold.

'Shropshire, babes, fucking Shropshire. Want another drink?'

Bottle number two and Gio was getting very touchy-feely. I'd come right up; I was as stoned as a fart.

'Why we stay here?'

'Darling, we don't have to stay anywhere. Let's fuck off – drink up first.'

We finished the bubbly in doubly quick time and headed out: it was still early. My pager went off with party info, perfect timing. I suggested the Westwood and Katharine

Hamnett parties; thought about them again and decided I couldn't be arsed poncing over to Covent Garden for the new spin on a Westwood bondage–mini-crini. I certainly didn't give a shit about what Hamnett's next T-shirted-non-bleached-right-on-cotton message was. We aimed up Shaftesbury Avenue for Lowlife instead.

London clubs are where it's all really at – Kinky Gerlinky, the Wag on Thursdays, Café de Paris on a Wednesday night, Legends and Taboo – they're all major gigs for the inveterate clubber. Ecstasy is new and very big news; I felt an inverted thrill when my Chinese E-dealer friend (***reality check three***: since when has any E-dealer been a friend?) became one of the first pushers to be busted for dealing in Britain. I mean, how cool is the glamour of a test case or the kudos of being able to say, 'I was nearly there'? Well, I was. It was the blasé-blah satisfaction of being in the know and the first, no matter how vicariously. We were Radio Rental for it, desperately seeking celebrity by association no matter how gassy the premise. It was like the *Marchioness* disaster. How many prats have been claiming to be guests at that party these last few weeks? According to the word going around town now, there are several hundred fake invitees (all of whom were never going to catch, let alone miss, the boat) who are finding it possible to glean esteem through having not drowned in the Thames.

It was miserable self-importance. Spurious association and bogus friendship with those in the know governs the entire scene. Forget Taboo unless you're on nodding terms at least with Trojan or Leigh, and the same applies with Gerlinda and her eponymous Kinky. And me? I know the lot, just look in my Filofax. The clubs are as greedy for second-hand prowess as the punters who frequent them – and it never comes much more second-hand than I do. Micro-celebrities are a speciality: it's impossible to go anywhere and not meet up with Martin Degville of Sigue Sigue Sputnik: the man is everywhere. Lowlife (a decommissioned church injected with glamour by a blond preppy Yank called Ding Ding fresh from the Area club in NYC) was making the biggest splash. It spearheaded the eighties revolution in West End clubs employing DJs Paul Oakenfold (fresh from Schoom), Gary (Aceeed) Haseman and Sasha; it was the only place to be. Gio and I rocked up the avenue – pissed and stoned – to the club. It was happening, and, there again, so was I.

We swanned past the ropes and the bouncers and the hundred or so hopefuls outside all straining to catch the eye of whoever had a clipboard (and thus guest-list Nirvana). There was never any trouble, it was like I owned the place. Past the cashiers, nodding, saying quick hellos, I was hardly ever out of there. We headed straight upstairs through crowds desperate to force themselves into the VIP room. Michael was on the door.

'Ahh. Mrs Jones, we've missed you, come on in.'

I was generally a Mrs although on occasion the grander title of Empress kicked in. It was one of those campy little things, an accolade, really, that was only bestowed on a couple of others and myself. We left dozens crammed on the stairs praying for an *entrée*, and slid inside. The VIP room was the inner sanctum for those who were regarded as cool, happening and worth having around. It was also a place to drink unlimited quantities of pink Laurent Perrier – and never pay for it. The best perk of being a scene-queen means you pay for nothing. It's free entry and free booze and inflatory air-kisses and E and much, much more champagne. Gio lapped it up. Mark, the manager, came over with the first of the evening's coke, another little something that was never paid for as a matter of principle.

'Mrs Jones, if you'd follow me, please . . .'

Lowlife was essentially hetero but for a tiny hard core of gay regulars who had brought in a great dollop of camp that the straight guys perversely adored.

'No excuses now, follow me, dear.'

Mark, who couldn't have been straighter if he'd tried, had adopted a deep-rooted campness that he found impossible to shake off. That and a pretty amazing coke habit to boot. We slipped upstairs to the offices and chopped out huge chalky lines of Charlie while watching the police cars hurl themselves around Cambridge Circus.

'Ah, the Empress Jacquelyn is here, and who does she have with her tonight?'

A sad old faggot (well, sadder than me) was trying to gate-crash my coke-fest and muscle in on novelty-caterpillar-torpedo man. He could go fuck himself and keep his itchy hands off Gio. Being geed up on E, a healthy sloosh of booze and a few lines of coke meant only one thing: invincibility. That's the great thing about immoderate amounts of drugs. Your fried mind believes you're unbeatable.

'The Duchess Veee Jay. Jet-lagged again?'

Veee Jay, predictably a DJ, had been a pop star once and he still reckoned he was. On top of his tiny Indian head he had an oversized quiff that had grown bigger and bigger as his celebrity had ebbed and receded – like some sort of inverse thermometer. It was now outstandingly large, fame quotient approaching zero. Veee ('that's V triple E, darling' – he'd be lucky to get one tonight) also had an amazing capacity to suffer the aforementioned lag. By my reckoning the last airborne trip he'd made was two years ago in '87, so his current state of exhaustion made him a major medical miracle.

'Yes, dahling, I flew in today, can't tell you how shattered I feel. Any chance of a line?'

There was a resounding 'Fuck off.' Neither Mark nor I was letting anyone, especially Veee, get in on our particular act. Gio looked on, impressed, but blew his cool by having a coke-laden ball of snot slip down towards his lip.

'Sweetie, if you ain't goin' to do it you can always give it to me.'

'Veee, I've told you already, fuck off, I'll sort you out later . . .'

Veee vanished, Gio licked his upper lip and the most expensive bogey in the world was gone. We were rocking.

Back downstairs the VIP was heaving. Veee, now with NBF gay porn star Fluff Reynolds, looked as if he was close to heaving too. His penchant for nasty peach schnapps topped with Bollinger would be enough to make the most hardened alky puke, even Veee. There was the funny geezer with a scar: he looked like a classic hoodlum, with his rolls of notes and splashy girlfriends but he was a pussycat, really. Gangsters were fashionable: they adored the sparkle of the regulars and the regulars loved the cachet of a crim. I once met a *Blue Peter* presenter who claimed her dad was an accountant for the Krays – now that's pushing credibility too far. Gio and I carried on drinking the pink.

'It's a beautiful ring.'

'I know, darling, fancy you remembering.'

'No, on your finger, is a beautiful ring.'

Gio's lazy eyes had alighted on what might conceivably pass as a serious rock. A ten-carat cubic zirconia sat not a little ostentatiously on my pinkie.

'It full of fire, is a special.'

Not wanting to detract from my fake credentials and the even more bogus jewel, I gave a knowing how-vulgar-of-you-to-mention-my-exceptional-diamond-ring type of look. Change subject.

'Do you reckon you're ready to leave?'

'Where we go?'

'Back to mine?'

'Ees OK.'

'I know, darlin', they're fab, let's have another.'

Another tab each, and Gio and I were off, into the night and our heads, not forgetting one last line with Mark.

'I'd say you were ACE, mate . . .'

ACE, alcohol, cocaine and ecstasy, and yes, I was . . . most nights.

We stumbled out of Lowlife, turned the corner into Greek Street and got into one of the mini-cabs driven by the Swahili fellas. We drove back to the flat and fell into bed, coked, E'd and fucked up.

HOME LIFE

'Hell*ooo*, darling. Where have you been then, you naughty boy?'

'Hi, Patrick, don't even ask, I'm shagged.'

'Thought you ought to know that the unlovely Max and his putrid Villy have been looking for you. *Sooo* has some dyke rabbi and I've had an absol*ooo*tely charming call from the *sweetest* undertaker's. Going to tell me what's going on?'

'Louis has died, and I've been roped into arranging his funeral, along with Max and Pedro and all those people you love . . .'

'What did he die of? Stagnation?'

'Give it a break, Pat. Does it matter? It was something to do with his lymphs. Cancer. It wasn't Aids, if that's what you're after.'

'Darling, and there's the rub of it. He never really had a chance to catch it now, did he?'

'Patrick, you can be such a bitch, the poor bugger's dead. I've pissed off his parents, though.'

'Why?'

'Well, it's not so much the organising, I think it's the timing. We should have been a little quicker in the ground. He's got traditional Jewish folks and it's been four days since he pegged it.'

'Well, *daaa*rling, you'd better hurry then, for their sake as well as yours. You don't want this to get in the way of the party at the weekend now, do you?'

Patrick is a lovable shit. He doesn't really mean what he says, it's his way. He's campy and has the knack of making a salient point savagely. Nothing is sacred, but it doesn't mean that he doesn't care. I always thought it was because he's incredibly posh. He's the supreme master of the self-assured *faux pas*, and won't or can't acknowledge his solecism. It's easy to tell he's from the top drawer: he always smokes when eating. He never puts a fag out, no matter what he's scoffing; there's an art to that that has to be congenital. But Patrick, for all his sharp peculiarity, is a love. He devised a campaign of Mindless Benevolence – paying anonymously for strangers. It was a great thing to do in a cinema queue.

'*Twoooo* tickets for *Steel Magnoooolias*, please. And you see that woman wearing the woolly hat four behind us? I'll pay for her as well, and please don't say it was me. This has to be anonymous.'

The result: one slightly confused but happy patron.

He does it in bars too. Rounds of drinks mysteriously appear on tables of complete strangers, not so that he can introduce himself and pick up whoever it is – it's his unique philanthropy. And even though his reaction to Louis dying sounded unforgivably vile, he wasn't.

'*Daaa*rling, are you sure you're OK? Can I help you with anything?'

It was his way and I loved him for it.

* * *

I did some high-octane phoning, firstly to Heavenly Body, the undertaker's, then Max, the curio-queen and his coterie, poor old Louis's parents up north and anyone else who'd listen.

'Hello, Gordy, it's Jake. The funeral is tomorrow, I hope that's OK . . . Yes, I know you feel strongly about his sexuality, I think you're the only one who ever has . . . But you can't say that, you really can't, not in front of his parents.'

Gordy Goldstein was forced to take an oath and promise solemnly not to mention that Louis was a poofter.

Gabby was determined to provide some sort of monument for Louis and she was adamant that she should bring it along to the graveside. 'I'm an artist, you know, I really need to see how the piece fits in with the other works. I feel I need to visit the site.'

'Fine, Gabby, whatever, but I genuinely believe that all the other works might just be gravestones, with the odd angel and a few crucifixes. Don't get too excited, it's hardly the type of event the Saatchis will turn up to.'

I had managed to get the event on the fast track as well as extract a promise from Erin that she would come too, even though she had hardly known Louis. It was all set, miraculously, for the next afternoon. I could chill.

'Jake *daaaa*rling, Gio on the phone for you. Hurry up now . . .'

'Thanks Pat. Hello?'

'Hello, Jake?'

'Yeah, howya doin'?'

'Is not good. I 'ave problem.'

'Like what?'

'A sex problem.'

'And . . .'

'I 'ave test the other day and is a problem for me, maybe you.'

'What test? Aids?'

'No, is not Aids.'

'Syphilis?'

'Eh, no, is not syphilis . . .'

'Then, darling, it's bound to be a spot of gonorrhoea.'

'*Si.*'

'Thank fuck.'

Gonorrhoea hardly rated as a tremor on the Richter scale of sexually transmitted diseases, although it depended on where you had it. Apart from the obvious orifice where it might make an unwelcome guest appearance, it did, once, pop up in my throat. The doctor at the clap clinic was most impressed. 'I've never seen it there before, that's very unusual. Do you mind if I show some of my students?'

The indignity of being in this exclusive club was one thing, but having a gang of three therapeutic virgins scrutinising my screech was something else. I was getting tetchy. I didn't much like being a pathological misfit. 'Contrary to received opinion I'm not Linda Lovelace and this isn't *Deep Throat*. Why don't you guys find something useful to do and go back to your *I-Spy Book of Ebola*.'

They did.

'Well, what fabulous news, Gio, you really know how to cheer a girl up.'

'I sorry. You want to meet me for drink tonight?'

'Darling, I'd love to, but I think not. We don't want any cross-infections, do we? Get yourself cleaned up, like I'm going to, and we'll speak at the weekend. There's a fab party on Saturday if you'd like to come.'

Thursday was panning out beautifully. Clap clinic in the morning and, provided I wasn't kept waiting too long, Louis's funeral in the afternoon; which meant, of course, another day off work. I was not going to be popular.

I called Erin. 'It feels that nothing's going my way at the mo.'

'What's the matter, Jakey?'

'I think I've got a spot of clap off Gio.'

'Jake, what are you trying to prove?'

I hadn't thought I was trying to prove anything, but it did feel as if the world had slipped out of gear. My sphere had always been indulgent but now it had taken on a markedly new spin; it was faster. Was I losing my grip?

'You know what, Jake? Let's you and me take off. Let's sod off out of London and have a weekend together. Just the two of us.'

'I don't think I can, babes. I've got a party on Saturday.'

'You can miss one poxy party, Jake.'

'Nope, we'll do it the next weekend, I promise. Are you still on for Louis's funeral? You know I'd really appreciate it if you came.'

'Of course I'll be there, but do something for me, Jake. Cool it a little, huh? I don't want you burning out on me. I need you as well.'

INTERMENT

Highgate Cemetery is very handy for Gospel Oak but it is not handy for the VD clinic in Charlotte Street. I arrived at Louis's do five minutes late, fashionably so in some circles, maybe, but a bit naff at a funeral. I felt like a bride as the entire congregation turned to watch little old me try to slip in unobtrusively between Patrick and Erin, who had rather nicely saved me a seat – it was a sell-out occasion. I didn't look like the blushing bride and I didn't look like I was headed for the despatch of a dear friend either. They'd kept me waiting at the clinic for ages so on my release I'd no option other than to leap into a cab and head straight for the service. I was still in my butch leather skirt and long felt jacket (well, at least they were black and grey respectively). I thought the skirt was just the right side of masculine. In fact, the outfit looked rather good – a little early-eighties Jean-Paul-Gaultieresque maybe, but stylish. Louis's mum and dad glared from the front, the myopic rabbi beamed (probably thought I was a local lezzer because of my get-up), Max and Pedro looked skywards and Gabby sighed audibly. I teetered in (the skirt was a bit tight around the ankles) and sat down. I was pleased to see that Pedro had settled on Shaker simplicity. Louis was in a pine box.

'We are here today to celebrate the life of Louis Cantor, a complicated man, whose outlook on life, even during his long illness, was always gay and optimistic.'

She had to do it: she just had to get the G-word in somehow.

'Although a bachelor throughout his life, Louis was loved by many, as can be seen here today in the congregation.'

Yes, it could. Two poofy antiques dealers in some rather fetching pastel shades, a couple of fairly obvious fag-hags, Gabby being dramatic in a hideous hat, seven dozen chums of Dorothy, and me, Patrick and Erin. Louis had just been outed to his parents at his own funeral. What did it matter now? He was dead, wasn't he?

We headed down the hill for the graveside, Louis making a break for it on an expandable chrome trolley with two muscle Marys from Heavenly Body trotting alongside, trying to give the cortège a little dignity. They tried, but failed. Gabby, Pedro and Max (now with their little Villy in a matching pastel bow) had started dabbing their eyes theatrically. Looming above the plot was something large and covered in black velvet. Gabby's sculpture, I guessed. As the Heavenly Body boys lowered Louis into the ground I felt tears well up. It was suddenly the most terrible, empty, final thing. Louis was dead. He was in that ugly box. He'd gone for ever. Erin gripped my arm as if I was a three-year-old ready to dash out on to the street. It felt surprisingly tight.

Gabby came to the fore. 'This is for Louis, a flame of life, a flame for his life.'

She whisked away the black velvet to reveal the most extraordinary piece of sculpture ever positioned in a graveyard. Think Henry Moore blob with hole, now think sphincter, now add dildo. Louis was going to get it more in death than he'd ever had it in life, from here to eternity with a lump of pornographic pottery above his head. He really was fucked. I gasped and giggled helplessly with Patrick and Erin at the phallic memorial. Rabbi Goldstein was in raptures, I could hear it in her voice: she was delighted. She became quite garrulous; we tried to stifle our laughter.

Louis's mum rather liked it: 'Maybe we could get another for us, Melvyn. We don't have nothing planned as yet.'

It was a national disgrace that the Saatchi brothers weren't there; it was funeral as art installation.

We walked away from the graveside, me arm in arm with Erin and Patrick.

'*Daaa*rling, don't you think leather is a bit much for this type of thing? Now tell me, *hoooow* did you get on at the clap clinic?'

'How do you expect, Pat? I won't know anything for a few days.'

Pedro interrupted: 'Yoohoo, we're off for tea and cakes down the road at the dearest little coffee shop. It's Max's favouwite, you know. Are you coming?'

'Do we have any option? Oh, Pat, I just hope I haven't got it in my throat this time.'

A crack team from the Czechoslovakian army ran Café Beethoven; at least, that's where the heavily accented, briskly efficient, lemon-faced waitresses looked like they had originated. This was fortunate, because we needed waiting staff with a military background to help drill the many mincing mourners who made up the numbers. There were a few tables set aside at the back for the funeral party and a gangway leading through Beethoven's regulars to more tables on the street outside for the overflow. We were lucky: we had the weather for it. Apart from the obligatory sarnies there was a surprisingly sumptuous array of cakes and pastries. I'd never associated chocolate éclairs with interment before. Pat, Erin and I found a table right at the back. Erin, the darling, had predicted that the occasion would be teetotal and had come armed accordingly. A bottle of vodders was surreptitiously opened and extra large ones poured into the soft refreshments.

'*Daaaaa*rling, thought you might need a little of this too.'

Patrick, double bless, had brought along a gram. After knocking back a couple of large shots, a communal trip to the loo was instigated. The re-entry from the bog of two ultra-refreshed queens and girlfriend didn't go down well with the waitress who caught us. I could tell she was disgusted, not because we were taking coke (she had no idea) but because of our obviously loose morals.

We were ready for another drink, but the booze had disappeared.

'It's got to be here somewhere, Erin. Did you put it in your bag?'

'I'm telling you, Jake, it's gone. Patrick, it's not behind your jacket, is it?'

Louis's mum, never, ever the drinking kind, had wisely

taken to alcohol in her instant of need and, not being familiar with Blue Label, was getting almightily pissed. *Haut* café society in NW5 was shocked, as were Max and Co. by the inebriated antics of a devastated woman. 'I never thought I'd see this. I've buried Louis. I've put my child in the ground. Do you understand? I've buried my child.' Louis's dad tried to comfort her, and she seemed to drift into a suppressed grief.

Patrick picked up his jacket. 'Erin, Jake, I think we should go now.'

As we got up to move Louis's mother found her voice again. She put on a cabaret: she'd become a drunk singing sad, smashed lyrics, virulently angry at still being alive. We left them there – shocked locals, a hundred mourners, disturbed bric-à-brac queens and an empty, wretched woman trying to figure out why her life had been quite so deceitful and unkind.

WORK

My continued absence at work cheesed off my boss, Richard, immensely. 'Jake, you've got to shape up. I mean, for God's sake, you've only been in one day this week. I couldn't give a damn about funerals or doctor's appointments so don't bother telling me about them.'

'Richard, I'm sorry, but I didn't exactly ask Louis to peg out. I'm in now, what more do you want?'

'For you to actually appear as if you're doing some work here. Is that too much to ask?'

Richard loved me; he didn't fancy me – God knows, I didn't fancy him – but he did have this caring-older-brother thing with me. He had done since the first day I worked there. We were both middle-class white boys – well, at least I was, Richard was the older version – who had done the art-school trip because no one else would have us. We'd both, at different times, received poor degrees in the finer arts from Camberwell. That made us Old Cambodians. But the biggest differences between us were in temperament and looks. Richard was very tall, very plump and extremely sweaty. He had the type of excess body fat that would engulf a finger should he be pressed with one – rather like prodding a condom full of cake-mix. He was an ex-hippie who still looked as if he was capable of knitting his own lentils, but in reality he was just a lazy closet capitalist. His sole aspiration was to make big money without anyone noticing, an ambition he only ever half realised – no one paid him any attention. His business, Bee Joux, otherwise known as BJ or, inevitably, Blow Job, was a fashion company. It retailed belts and bags and big ugly junk jewellery, and I really was its designer. But let's not give this any hype: the whole set-up was pretty low rent and tawdry. The jewels were more likely to appear on the lobes of some 36–24–36 tabloid lovely than ever they were on a *bona fide* model. There was much excitement in BJ when the barmaids in *Corrie* and *EastEnders* wore the same Bee Joux earrings in the same week. It was that kinda place.

My cutting-edge bijou bollocks hadn't been a total lie to Gio. I was putting a collection together that consisted primarily of Day-Glo. Huge lurid pink lids for lugs, puce beads, acid yellow bangles and rancid orange elastic belts were figuring large. I was also thinking black leather and chrome.

'Let's do something along the Corbusier line.'

'Like the brandy, darlin'?'

'No, the friggin' architect.'

Mock-croc, fake snake and phoney ponyskin, printed up to look like leopard and zebra, were going to be this season's big fashion statements; at least, they were according to me. It was as if I was on a one-man mission to make the world especially ugly. I'd got an entire army of YOPs – Youth Opportunity Placements from the dole office working at slave-labour rates – mindlessly gluing fluorescent glitter on to anything I could think of and quite a lot of stuff besides that would have been better left virgin. Satchels and bucket bags were about to be reinvented: they were going to be hard, tough accessories for urban cowgirls. The *pièce de résistance* was the 'Kill Your Granny' belt, a huge strip of industrial rubber studded and chained to oblivion, the very last word in fetish chic. If the truth were known it was probably heavy-duty pervs who purchased the more esoteric of my gear. Who else in their right mind would want it? Rubber belts in all their hideousness proved surprisingly popular. Their success was borne out by the string of concessionary shops that Richard had dotted across London. They all purveyed the Jake Jones/Richard Hoster brand of tat. So I guess that proved that someone somewhere bought it.

That Richard had started a company to produce such exotica had always been a bit of a puzzle to me. Ultimately he was a proper kind of guy, imbued with public-school tradition – which, of course, made him a little retarded when it came to deeper communication. He was very good at in-jokes, though, especially with the BJ élite – me. It seemed to me that, for him, tacky jewellery and crappy belts were a cop-out. He was the type of bloke cursed only to show potential, which was illustrated by him forever referring to his successful and famous contemporaries in the hope that some of their magic might rub off on him. Not that I'd do anything as crass.

'You must have seen the work of Eva Bergstrom in the V and A, Jake.'

'I can't say that I have.'

'It's interesting stuff, acrylic bands set with diamonds.'

'No, I really haven't.'

'I'm surprised, Eva's a very good friend of mine.'

These conversations always left me feeling a tad confused. Why should his having a good friend who stuck precious stones into plastic ensure that I'd seen any of the artefacts they'd produced? It didn't matter to Richard: it was his only chance to show off his impeccable contacts.

'Who is Eva Brainstorm anyway?'

'No need to be clever, Jake. She's a very talented jeweller. It wouldn't do you any harm to take a look at her stuff.'

Richard and his friends: he had a list of them. There was a bloke who did stuff for Jasper Conran and a woman who had designed a range of something for Tiffany no less. And, yes, they ended up in my *filo* bit too. God only knows why, I put it down to compulsion. We all seemed to collect numbers.

'Eva Barnyard, right. I'll look out for her, Richard. Her work sounds fab.'

GIO'S PLACE

'Erin, babes, it's me. Hello? Answer the phone.'

The one thing that bugged me about Erin was that she never answered her phone.

'Erin, pick up the phone, will you? It's me, Jake.'

I might be neurotic and collect names like an urban train-spotter, but Erin is pathological about screening calls. I hung up and called her straight back. This drove her wild because the answerphone wouldn't click back in and the phone carried on ringing.

'Jake?'

'At long bloody last. What are you up to later?'

'No plans as yet.'

'Fancy a girly night out and meeting my new fella?'

This was always a bit of a trauma, not for Erin or the new man but for me. I needed Erin to like them. If she didn't, I invariably got rid of them. This wasn't because she required me to dump them – I don't think she knew I did this – it was because, deep down, the person I really wanted to be with, perversely, was Erin.

'Yes, Jake, I'd love to. Where do you want to meet?'

'We'll see you at Lowlife at midnight.'

I had decided that it was time not only to hook back up with Giovanni, I was going to promote him to introduction-with-Erin status. Gio lived in a flat in Bermondsey. Walking into the estate was a bit like entering a set for some gritty, Britty black-and-white genre movie. Any minute now a kitchen sink followed by a young Rita Tushingham would come hurtling out of a top-floor window to mug me with earthy reality. It looked as if some bloke from the special-effects department in Elstree had given the flats the once-over because there was no way a real place could look like this. ***Reality check four***: there was, and this was it. It was a red-brick tenement that had been shoved up quickly in the late forties, a precursor to multi-level car parking, with about as much comfort. No lift – not that you'd risk using it if there was – just badly lit, filthy stairs dotted with junkies, old syringes and rubbish. It seemed strangely familiar. It was. It was the daylite-low-rent-apocalyptic-urban-trash version of Lowlife on a Friday night. I found Gio's door.

'Hi, Jake. Come in.'

The flat looked marginally better than outside: it had a better class of mess. Old bikes, piles of free papers that had never made it to a bin and ancient paint tins littered the hall. The latter were congealed in a new Dulux pastel colour: white-with-a-hint-of-cat-pee. It was bareboarded and grim. The living room had been furnished with the last syllable of Habitat and had that shagged-in, puked-in, murdered-in feel that I imagine most serial killers would feel at home with. I was showing as much interest in the surroundings as Prince Philip might in a black lesbian mothers' drop-in centre.

'Come and see my room.'

We went up what might easily have passed as medieval steps to Gio's bedroom, and respite. Thank God for Italian queens. Poor, yes, but stylish. He'd created an entire aquarium of outlandish octopi and assorted seafood, a Gothic fishcotheque swirling around his bedroom walls. What couldn't Gio do with an indelible marker and a couple of tubes of acrylic paint? It looked fab. Gio was fab. Sod the clap-clinic results. We fell back into bed.

Waking up in the early evening in Gio's fish tank wasn't quite the happy experience I'd imagined. I was convinced that his flat was the model for Dennis Nilsen's place and I was outta there.

'Gio, do you fancy a night out?'

'Yes, I like.'

'Great, let's go to Lowlife then. Hurry up, you'll be meeting my best friend Erin.'

[illegible]

[illegible] for [illegible]

[illegible] ... [illegible] out [illegible]

[illegible] in [illegible] better than [illegible] [illegible] for [illegible] of the [illegible] [illegible] one of these [illegible] was [illegible] [illegible] cross the [illegible] was [illegible] side [illegible]

[illegible]

[illegible] ack. You [illegible] Sunday morning [illegible]

I [illegible] ght for a moment [illegible] hard had [illegible] and [illegible] found [illegible] workshop [illegible] me. I could [illegible] mounded [illegible] les and [illegible] ing his way [illegible] ength and [illegible] rd [illegible]

OPPORTUNITY KNOCKS

'Darling, *daaa*rling, the phone. Wake up. It's the fucking *phooone* for *yooou*. Jake, will you please wake up?'

Patrick had been hammering on the door and hollering for a couple of minutes, his clatter only just registering in my foggy head. 'Mmm? Phone? Yep, one sec.'

I'd put on one of those yes-I-know-what-I'm-doing-and-I'm-wide-awake voices, even though I was still on the sleepy side of catatonic.

'Hello.'

'Jake, it's Richard.'

Panic, I was late again. Buggering buggery. It must be eleven, fuck. Think of an excuse, there must be something. ***Reality check five***: it was the weekend. ***Reality check six***: it was Sunday.

'Yeah, hi, Dick. You do know it's Sunday morning, don't you?'

I had thought for a moment that Richard had lost the plot and was to be found seething in his sweatshop with no staff, especially no me. I could see him surrounded by antiquated diamanté bangles and coiled belts clawing his way to the phone ready to spit venom and fire the bastard absentee designer.

'Yes, Jake, I do know, sorry it's early. I was wondering, would you want to go on holiday?'

He must have flipped – or was this just an elegant way of firing me?

'What are you talking about?'

'I was wondering if you'd like to go on holiday to Palermo for a week, all expenses paid.'

I was dumbstruck. Since when did any twenty-four-year-old gay guy not want to go on holiday? And since when did anyone not want it for free? 'Richard, what are you trying to tell me?'

'It's quite simple. Do you want a free holiday or not? What's so difficult about the question?'

I had been thrown completely off track. I had anticipated being elbowed out, but instead I was being offered a mini-break.

'I mean, yeah, but why? When?'

'That's the catch. You'd have to leave tomorrow, then come back in a week's time.'

I wasn't sure what to make of Richard's largess. Of course I'd like a holiday, but why me? Images of dodgy drug deals and Mafia cocaine swept through my mind. At long last, Richard was going to make some money. If he couldn't make it with necklaces he'd do it with narcotics. I had visions of swapped suitcases and kilos of coke Sellotaped to my quaking bod. There'd be Neapolitan men with dark specs and *grappa*-breath shadowing me on scooters merrily snatching handbags from old ladies as they cruised after me through the Roman streets. There'd be Venetian guns and live rounds, for goodness' sake. Mafia bosses with violin cases would be waiting for me in pools of light at the bottom of dark Milanese stairwells. I'd probably end up in a sweaty Italian prison for a lot longer than a week. (Twenty-two years seemed to have a more pertinent ring to it. For a second, Italian prison seemed rather tempting – imagine being holed up with dozens of Giovannis. Then again, perhaps not.) And what of the Cosa Nostra? I guessed an unmarked grave on a Florentine hillside might be more their style. No, suddenly I wasn't too keen on the idea. I knew this was dodgy, but Richard, for all his failings, had never struck me as the international-drug-trafficking type.

'Dick, I don't know what this is all about, but even I can smell a rat. What are you trying to get me into?'

'It's nothing odd. Really.'

'You sure it's not cocaine smuggling or something equally terrible?'

'Have you quite lost it? Don't be so bloody stupid. I want you to help a friend of mine. She's not very well, a bit poorly, and needs a chum to help get her to Italy. You'd be a travelling companion.'

'But why me?'

'Well, she was supposed to go with another chum who, er, dropped out unexpectedly right at the last minute. I thought you'd be able to go, and you need a break.'

I still wasn't sure why me, and I still wasn't convinced about Richard's altruistic motives.

'She's an old friend, you'll like her. She's been very badly let down. I just wanted to help her get away. As a bonus you'll have the opportunity for a bit of fun. All you've got to do is carry her luggage – she's not capable. It's no big deal.'

'And we'd be going to Italy for a week. I'd carry her bags, do my own thing and then come back?'

'Exactly.'

'And that's it?'

'Yep.'

'And it's a freebie?'

'All expenses paid.'

'Where'd we stay?'

'Vulcano, it's an island off Sicily.'

'And that's it? Bags and holiday?'

'Yes, for goodness' sake. You'll get a hundred quid for your trouble too.'

'Sure, I'll do it.'

The whole venture was beginning to sound pretty fab. A week's holiday for free. Going tomorrow wasn't a prob. I'd bowl up to Vulcano, hang around and check out the talent. Richard interrupted my reverie: 'Travel pretty lightly, won't you? You'll have to carry Eva's juice machine as well.'

A juice machine was not going to stifle my new enthusiasm for this hol. Nor was travelling light. I had an entire wardrobe of flimsy chiffon and transparent silk gauze that could roll up into nothing. I saw it now – another opportunity at the end of the summer to wear those yummy, frothy clothes. I had done my rapid mental pack, my small leather suitcase was already being checked in. No, it wasn't, I still hadn't unpacked it after a trip I'd made to Paris. I was nearly sussed.

'What do I do about tickets?'

'You'll meet Eva tomorrow at Heathrow, she'll have everything.'

'Aren't you going to be there?'

'I don't think so, no. I'm too busy. You'll find her easily. Nip along to the Alitalia desk in terminal three at twelve noon, check in and you're off.'

'How will I recognise her?'

'You won't miss her, she's Eva Bergstrom, for goodness' sake. She'll be there with a few friends by the check-in desk – it's not that bloody big.'

The name rang a bell, but for the life of me I couldn't think why. I made a mental note to check my Filofax: I had a hunch that Louis might have known her.

Richard hung up, and I'd woken up. 'Patrick – Pat? Guess what? I'm off again. I'm going to Vulcano.'

'*Wheeeere*, *daaaa*rling?'

'An island off Italy with some woman who's not well. I've become a sherpa. I've got to carry her luggage to the hotel then chill for a week. Richard asked me to go. Cool, isn't it?'

'*Daaa*rling, you are doing well on the travel front, *aaaaren't* you?'

'Well, that's me clear of having to go to Max and Pedro's doggy shower.'

'Their what?'

'They've got another filthy pup as a friend for Villy and I've been cordially invited to christen the bloody thing with them.'

'Who's the father?'

'I've no idea, but I'm sure either Pedro or Max will eventually give the game away by lactating. And now I'll never know.'

'*Daaaa*rling, that makes me puke. Now, are you going to

spend all day chatting with me or are you going to pop back into your bedroom and see to your guest?'

In my post-cocaine-done-in-from-last-night haze and phone-call-this-morning-God-I'm-going-on-holiday whirl I'd quite forgotten the new squeeze. I jumped back into bed for a celebratory bonk with Giovanni before ejecting him on the pretext of serious travel business.

'Erin, babes, it's me.'

'Jakey, I'm still asleep from last night. Thanks for a great time. I have to say your little chum Giovanni is lovely. Let's hope you hang on to him this time.'

'Thanks, darling, but listen to this. I'm off to Italy for a week.'

'What?'

'Dick has asked me to go as a favour for a mate of his. I leave tomorrow, won't be back till next Saturday so I reckon our weekend away together will have to wait.'

'Jake, you are one jammy sod. What is it with you? I thought he was about to sack you because you're never in. Why's he sending you off on a jolly?'

The edited highlights of the freebie were recounted once more.

'Jake, have a fabulous time. Make sure you send me a postcard, and send one to the lovely Gio too. Be nice to him. And let me know as soon as you get back, we'll have a night in together. Love you, Jake. Don't be gone too long. 'Bye, baby.'

That was rather satisfactory. She really liked Gio and wasn't even vaguely upset about me not going away with her the next weekend. It was Erin to a T. Who could have a better pal?

'Patrick, I'm going to Lowlife tonight, fancy coming along?'

'Is it open on a Sunday?'

'It's a new thing they're doing tonight. Mark wants to open a new section. I thought I'd pop along to celebrate my trip, are you coming?'

'Well, why not? Let's send you *ooorf* in style . . .'

We got a cab and headed into the West End. Lowlife was surprisingly busy.

'Mrs Jones, yoohoo. Oh, and Lady Patrick, what an honour.' Mark came over. 'Glad you're here, I'm opening the VIP's VIP and you, dears, are going to christen it.'

It was unusual for me to get two invitations to a christening in as many days. I was beginning to feel positively maternal.

'Come up into the organ loft. We've had the whole place fitted out, it's something else.'

Mark, Patrick and I nipped upstairs into the new room and found that Veee Jay and Fluff were already there. Bizarrely we'd got our own bouncer on the door – to stop *Blue Peter* presenters entering – and sole use of a waiter, who was now on an intense aerobic mission to try to keep up with the cry for champagne. The place looked amazing. Along the centre of the room ran a very long and very beautiful refectory table, and in one wall – overlooking the dance-floor fifty feet below – there were three specially glazed and soundproofed Gothic arched windows. The place even had its own sound system. It was rocking. Mark was feeling particularly generous and got the coke out for everyone. The Laurent Perrier was being poured in tidal quantities. We were going to get out of it in major style. ACE again. I had an idea. Any object that's long and flat and prominent can only mean one thing: a catwalk. I started striding up and down the table, briefly joined by Veee Jay who made a vain attempt at doing a Jerry Hall, but not well enough, and then decided on a more explicit entertainment. Fuck modelling, it was time for strip-tease. It was Gypsy-Rose-Lee-does-bad-burlesque drunken-deranged-faggot styley. I teetered around, a miracle considering the absence of heels, and hurled my attire to the floor. It was all very in, all very funny, all very cliquey, all drugged up and boozy. I fell off the table and struggled back into my kit, then went straight back to snozzing up more of Mark's gear.

More of the pink stuff and a lot more coke later, Patrick and I decided to nip off home. We were pushing through the throng at the door when someone said, 'Great show, mate.'

'What?' I was talking to a complete stranger.

'Yer show, top stuff.'

'What are you goin' on about?'

'The strip-tease, fuckin' great stuff.'

Reality check seven: it had been public. My cabaret had not been the private affair I'd thought. I, dopy eejit, had thought the VIP's VIP windows were mirrored. They were not. Five hundred disco bunnies had stopped dancing in the club below and had watched my entire performance. I was beginning to receive more appraisals of my night's work from the other punters. It really was time for a break. Patrick thought it hysterical; I was not best pleased.

'*Daaaa*rling, you're going off with a bang. I'm *suure* your little dance this evening opened quite a few eyes.'

'Let's go home, Pat.'

We took a cab back. I set my alarm, smoked a joint and crashed.

HEATHROW

I could hear Patrick in the flat. I guessed it must be about ten – no alarm, I must have extinguished it in my sleep – and for the life of me I couldn't remember last night. My head felt like a blank, a big empty hole, and I wasn't yet sure if it hurt. I lay there musing as to the severity of my imminent hangover. I was feeling awful without feeling sick, beyond the hangover stage, and headed towards a unique indisposition. Uncoordination was the very best I could hope for. If I just lay there, perhaps everything would be OK. Something felt uncomfortable: it was digging into my back. I fished out a depleted tube of KY, a small reminder of yesterday's fun with Gio, which, in my comatose state, I'd roosted on all night.

'Jake, aren't you up yet?'

It was Patrick shouting at me. I'd try to ignore him.

'You'll be very late if you don't get up now.'

'For what? I can't get up feeling like I do. Blow Blow Job. It will have to carry on without me. I need to sleep.'

'And Vul*caaaano*, my little sherpa belle?'

'Fuck. What's the time?'

Ten? It was nearly eleven. I fell into the bathroom and tried to locate signs of brain activity, which were not evident. The grey matter would need stimulation: it would need coffee, plenty of it, and a quick lick of the now empty coke wrapper, which was still in last night's trousers. Grab the knackered old suitcase and throw out the clothes from my last trip to make way for the gauzy bits for this one. Pick up passport and question the wisdom of wearing a Tom of Finland T-shirt that featured naked cowboys, thought better of it and ran out of the door. I caught the bus, then the tube. Found the Piccadilly line at King's Cross and sank back into sleep for the hour it would take to Heathrow. I was engulfed by a wave of nausea and for a scary moment I thought I might gag. I was not a well bunny. I caught my reflection opposite: I didn't look like one either. I fell back to sleep, soothed by the lurching of the train and repelled by the chronic body odour of the man sitting next to me.

I got to Heathrow at just gone twelve, not bad for someone who had, until recently, been contemplating the whole day in bed nursing a particularly tragic hangover. I wandered into terminal three – looking and feeling retarded – and found Alitalia and the desk for Palermo. I couldn't see Eva, but there again focusing on anything was a bit of a strain. I looked around and noticed a small group of people a little way off: one guy was looking about anxiously – it was obvious that he was waiting for someone. It had to be Eva and her posse.

I walked up to the bloke doing the looking. 'Are you with Eva?'

'Yes, and you must be Jake.'

There was a strange look on his face, a mixture of relief and distaste. I presumed he was giving me weird looks because of my toxic complexion. I was beginning to feel particularly fazed from the previous night.

'Come over, Jake, let me introduce you.'

I might have appeared odd, but I was nowhere near as supernatural-looking as she was. Her skin was yellowish and a bit plasticky. She had a bony face, neck, shoulders and arms, and a bulky lower half that looked as if it had been wrapped up in several layers of clothing. It was quite possible that her belly and legs were headed for the Arctic and the remaining 50 per cent was booked in for an anorexic fortnight in Benidorm.

'Hi, m' name's Jake, nice to meet you.'

She nodded and looked haughtily at me. 'Thank you for coming. I'll be with you in a minute, if you don't mind.'

Eva cut me dead and carried on chatting with her chums. They were obviously close friends, fussing over one another, Eva in the middle of it all. I was definitely not party to their cliquey gaggle so I sidled off towards the check-in desk wondering whether I might feel better if I threw up.

The lookout came trit-trotting over to me. 'Richard came up trumps, then.'

'Excuse me?'

'Richard managed to persuade you. I can only say thank you for coming to the rescue at such short notice.'

'It's cool, no probs.'

'No, really, thank you very much, it's very considerate of you. Now, it's vital that you have my number here and that you feel free to call me at any time. You must ring if there are any complications.'

My cocaine and champagne hangover went into suspended animation and the nausea was temporarily arrested. My brain was trying to click into gear. What was the guy telling me? I probably looked even more dim-witted than I had when I arrived.

'What do you mean, complications?'

'Eva's got cancer.'

'Eva, I believe, is poorly . . .' I was getting into my stride now. What was this bollocks? '. . . and that means the flu or a broken leg, a nervous breakdown even. It doesn't mean cancer.'

'I'm afraid that's what it is. She needs to rest while you're away. She needs to convalesce. I think it's better to be safe than sorry, don't you think?'

There was silence, at least there was between the dumpy guy and me. The terminal reeled around us.

'What the fuck are you going on about?'

'I mean, it's better for you to be prepared just in case of emergency.'

'I think it's safe to say we've got a bloody emergency now. You're telling me that we've got a terminal in terminal three, and I'm the silly git that's supposed to look after her.'

The harbinger didn't look remotely concerned. 'Jake, it's a bit late in the day to be making a fuss about it, isn't it?'

The messenger of doom looked improbably fatuous.

'We're very grateful for your help, but if you weren't up for this trip then you should never have agreed to go in the first place. Now, here is the hundred quid and here's your ticket.'

There were five dirty twenties in a reused B.T. envelope.

'Eva needs this trip badly. She's had a rough time of it. Now, let's make the most of it, shall we? Here's my number.'

I was stunned. I felt as if the trolleys and luggage and my graphically explicit hangover had marooned me. I felt sold down-river for a fifth of a manky monkey, which was now safely stuffed in my pocket.

I walked over to the leaving party. I guess now it was mentioned she did look ill, freaky-ill. What the hell was I supposed to do? Richard, the shit, had screwed me. Here I was, stuck at the airport with a group of handwashing strangers, a critical woman and third-degree crapulence. The bags were already checked in, apart from mine, a plane was about to take off towards a week of Mediterranean misery, and my idea of a free holiday was rapidly unravelling before me. Eva was ready to travel. I felt cornered. I'd promised I'd go, it was my name on the ticket and I didn't feel there was time to change my mind. There was no time. There was no option. Eva's chums were staring at me. It was a *fait accompli.* I guess I was going.

Eva was still chatting to her friends, a group of strangers eager to wave goodbye to me and, I was cottoning on fast, to wave a last goodbye to her. She turned towards me. 'Jake, you'd better check in your bag. We're already a bit late.'

I took the plunge, walked up to the Alitalia desk and handed over my passport and ticket. Then the entire group headed towards Departures. The strangers made cheery noises about seeing Eva in a week's time, squeaky-happy-clucky-let's-kid-ourselves-it'll-all-be-OK noises, and then they were gone. Eva shuffled – I walked slowly alongside – through the airport. We weren't about to start chatting or get into a jovial holiday spirit. Everything felt sour. We approached a security gate: I thanked God that I'd had the good sense to abandon the cocky T-shirt and leather skirt today. I put my hand luggage through the X-ray machine and walked through the metal-detector.

Eva didn't. I looked back to see what was happening and saw her arguing with one of the security guys.

'Would you please walk through the gate, Madam?'

'No, Madam bloody well won't.'

'I'm sorry, but all passengers have to go through the gate.'

'And I'm sorry but I absolutely will not. I don't want those rays zapping my body.' She had plunged straight into a monumental stand-off with a bloke ingrained with vocation value.

'The machine's harmless, Madam.'

'I don't care. I can't go through it – you'll have to search me by hand.'

A growling security woman joined in. She looked like an Eastern European Olympic-discus champion *circa* 1972, pumped up on adrenaline and steroids and with the first flush of a bum-fluffy moustache making its début. She wasted no time in frisking Eva.

I ignored the commotion and went to find my bag instead. It was then that it hit me – Eva and I were marked out from everyone else. I felt powerfully that we had been identified as the odd couple, definitely conspicuous; we were officially something different. She hobbled towards me, angry that she'd had to be searched; she was snotty and indignant. We walked slowly towards Duty Free in silence and sat in the adjacent café. I ordered the biggest diet Coke available – needing desperately to rehydrate – and Eva had a glass of hot water. She rifled through her bag and retrieved a small sachet, which she dipped into the beaker. Slowly the liquid went green and looked as if it might not smell too good. Eva's idea of tea was obviously more PC than PG. She was into evil Japanese infusions, bitter and, no doubt, very, very good for you. 'I take this because it's pure. That's why I wouldn't go through the X-ray machine. It wasn't pure.'

Who was I to argue? Did I care?

'I'll tell you now, I won't have anything impure around me. I'm fighting this disease from the inside so I don't need drugs and I certainly don't want rays.'

This talk of purity was a little worrying. She was beginning to sound as if she was a fully paid-up member of the master race. As for not having anything impure around her, I didn't want to shatter her tantric hallucination and introduce myself as being a fully Zen-free drugged-up zone.

'Do you understand this idea of purity, Jake?'

I looked at her blankly. She changed tack and started to tell me a little about her illness. 'It appeared five years ago. Just a few ugly cells in a smear.' After her cancerous cells had been diagnosed and treatment proffered she decided to go it alone and zap the unwanted guests with root juice and herbal infusions. She was, I thought, the type of woman who was obviously ready to commune with nature at the drop of a chickpea. Curing cancer with carrots and, I dare say, hate is a dangerously bucolic business. But, much to the surprise of the various medics at the Royal Free Hospital, she'd done rather well. She'd been expected to kick her balti years ago, but Eva wasn't ready to die. Oh, no, she was obstinate and very much in the process of living.

'We're going to Vulcano for a reason. There're the most amazing mud pools. I need to sit in them. The volcanic mud will help cleanse my body.'

Volcanic mud struck me as being a little more potent than the metal detector: I started to gamble on her going in for the hippie version of radiotherapy.

'It has to be natural. I haven't even taken an aspirin for this disease.'

Treating cancer with aspirin seemed a pretty novel idea: it was the inverse of treating a mild headache with smack. There again I could think of at least two people of my acquaintance who had never had a headache in their lives but still had a habit. The latter seemed preferable by far. The cancer, I was finding out, had spread to her stomach and – I was double-guessing – just about everywhere else. I left her sitting with her filthy green infusion and mooched into Duty Free.

I'd got a hundred quid to spend, I was thinking aftershave and vodka, and was pleasantly distracted by a fantastic offer on Clinique. There are certain types of shopping that only gay men can do successfully, and buying Clinique skin care in all seriousness is one of them. I had a last sashay through perfumes, picked up a family-sized bottle of Eau Sauvage then hacked over to the fag counter to buy four hundred Marly Lights – I could always say one of the cartons was Eva's. I went back to the café for the last cuppa, and then we headed towards the gate. Our brief conversation had died. I wasn't being told any more about her affliction, I wasn't being told anything. I surmised that Eva wasn't altogether happy with her travelling companion; I couldn't say that I was either. The two of us were silent, as if we were in a big sulk. We boarded.

Eva wrapped herself in one of those chic grey shawls (woven with so many scrotal hairs from some endangered species) around her shoulders. A *shatoosh*. Bless you. There was a bloke sitting in front of us reading the *Guardian*. Eva, still not speaking to me, moved suddenly, which was a bit of a shock: until then she had shown about as much sporting prowess as one of my elderly neighbours. She had spotted a large non-cheery headline about cervical cancer in the women's section (could it have been anywhere else?) and was ready to mug the geezer reading the paper in her attempt to get a hold of it. 'I'm sorry, but I have to see that, if I can just have that page? That's the one. Thank you,' she said.

She took the entire paper from him. She didn't look particularly grateful – she was behaving as if it were her right. Then she pored over the article, grumping. I tried to read as much as I could over her shoulder. The piece had been written by a woman who'd had a similar cancer to Eva's, but this woman had gone to hospital, had chemotherapy and eventually surgery. She had done it the traditional way; she'd done everything Eva hadn't. She was now a well woman, an alive woman, admittedly minus some of the bits that helped define her as such, but she was kicking none the less.

None of this impressed Eva: in fact, it pissed her right off. It was as if the woman in the paper had copped out in some way, as if she'd not done the right thing. She hadn't looked to nature and blind faith: she'd betrayed every other sufferer and spoiled herself with chemicals and an invasive surgeon's knife. There was only one way to deal with cancer, and it was Eva's way.

I wasn't about to argue: I was more taken aback by her intensity, her bloody-mindedness, her conviction. I decided to veer away from any conversation about chemicals and drugs, especially those of the class-A variety, as I had the feeling we wouldn't see eye to eye on the subject. Actually, I had the feeling that we weren't going to see eye to eye on anything much. I asked her tentatively if she'd been to Max's antiques shop. She glared at me.

COSA NOSTRA

At last we were talking. It wasn't chummy-worra-laff-can't-wait-till-we-land chatter, it was a much more basic communication. But it was something. The plane touched down in Palermo and I felt a buzz, a definite tickle of excitement. It was kinda weird feeling excited, when the journey had started so badly – or was I in the preliminary stages of losing my marbles and had forgotten just how dire the situation was? Nope, I was just happy to be in Palermo. Everyone on board shot off leaving Eva and me sitting behind. I was as desperate as anyone else to hurl myself to the front of the plane – I've never been cool at waiting my turn on touchdown – and only stayed seated at Eva's insistence. Once the aircraft was empty we disembarked like a couple of old biddies. The luggage was already on the carousel – that has to be a first for anyone – and knocking around by itself was the juice machine. ***Trolley awareness*** and off. I was itching to get going. I left Eva and went to find a cab, thought twice about taking it myself and leaving the invalid behind, but chickened out. I guess, after taking the flight, that was the second big mistake of the day.

As we drove into Palermo the light was fading but the city

was coming alive. My party antenna went on to automatic and twitched. Eva wasn't saying much, which suited me as I was already plotting my escape. Sure as hell, I was not going to be stuck with her all evening. I had conjured up an image of a local bar for later and, hopefully, detection of the regional speciality, whoever he was. The cab took us towards the railway station. Eva had been here before and knew of a place to stay that would be handy for the trains. We checked in. I can't say I was overwhelmed with her choice. Forget rustic-peasant-simplicity-darling-it's-so-cheap-yet-so-stylish-you'd-never-find-anything-like-this-at-home-in-Britain class of style-led accommodation. Think low-rent Bognor. I had thought that this type of hotel was unique to down-at-heel English seaside resorts, but I was wrong. It was bare lightbulbs and Formica, moth-bally and a bit sad. We checked into our separate rooms. Mine was down the corridor from Eva's. I was feeling thankful that Palermo was for just one night: the combination of sickness and poverty was not going to make for a great vacation.

I heard a thumping along the way. I looked out to see a guy from the hotel struggle to pull a spare bed out of Eva's room; she was directing the manoeuvres and was patently pissed off. I was having none of it: my job description was baggage-handler not interior-bloody-designer. She could make her own domestic arrangements. I had more important issues at hand, primarily along the lines of what I should wear. I threw on a voluminous silk shirt, which was just this side of being a blouse, a pair of handkerchief linen shorts that fell just below the knee and Indian sandals that rubbed my toes but looked gorge.

Eva found me in my room. 'Are you hungry yet, Jake?'

'I suppose so.'

'Well, that settles it. We'll eat local.'

Local was an understatement. We managed a left turn from the hotel and promptly sat down at a table in the trattoria next door. We were going to have pizza; it felt like an order. We sat below a huge tree, and while she studied the menu, I – being non-U – studied the men. Across the street was a gang of gorgeous natives who were sullenly kicking an old Coke can around the street. I'd never seen anyone pout while playing football before. I quickly considered taking sacred vows of allegiance and joining the local branch of the YMCA, the Young Mafioso Criminal Association – it couldn't be that difficult to get a complimentary membership, could it? We ordered and started to eat. I was surreptitiously trying to make eye-contact with my new friends while downing the red *molto pronto*; Eva was picking at her food and staring me out.

It didn't take too long for the Sicilian youth brigade to make an opening gambit, but it wasn't quite what I'd anticipated. They weren't playing the Beautiful Game with their can: it was a lot more aggressive. Loud yelps preceded the tin as it flew within feet of the table we were sitting at. Two kids pursuing it swerved away from us at the very last minute. It wasn't football; it was a bullfight. In retrospect I don't think they liked my shirt. I concede that, yes, maybe it was a little on the girly side but, hey, ever heard of irony? I'd – or, more to the point, we'd – become a laughing stock for the indigenous talent. We were the objects of silly jokes and teenage humour – at least that's what I understood to be the case because I couldn't speak Italian. The Coke can landed under the table and Eva looked even grimmer than before – a gurning miracle – while I was enjoying the whole show in my ignorant-slightly-drunken-I'm-on-holiday-let's-flirt-with-the-locals way.

I had another glass of wine, which was speedily followed by my first bollocking from Eva: 'I haven't come away to spend my time with an alcoholic, Jake. You drink far too much.'

I'd had a bottle of red – done stealthily, or so I had thought, as two half carafes. This was hardly a case for the Betty Ford Clinic. I considered opening my own establishment, the Betty O'Reilly Clinic: it would be a caring and understanding refuge that would provide teetotallers with a fully comprehensive grounding; alcohol and drug violation would be viewed in a positive light. The regime would start each morning with sherry trifles, wine-based sauces, cough medicine and mouthwash. After successfully completing the initial induction, patients would move on to Jell-O shots and, eventually, work up to a bottle and a half of vodders a day with a selection of soft, hard and dodgily obtained prescriptive narcotics thrown in for good measure.

But it wasn't my seemingly unlimited consumption of booze that was bugging Eva: my equally voracious smoking did her nut in too. What was she on and, more to the point, what was I in? I was a baggage-handler on holiday, she couldn't expect any more than that. I thought better of ordering more wine and didn't dare risk trying to bridge the cultural divide between half a dozen wannabe Mafiosi and myself. I went into best-behaviour mode and even then she complained.

We went back inside the hotel, Eva shuffling and me mincing. My night had been abruptly curtailed so I reconciled myself to having fun in Vulcano instead. I said goodnight to Eva.

'Before you turn in I would like you to make my sheets.'

'I'm sorry?'

'Could you please make up my sheets?'

'Your sheets? Didn't the chambermaid make the bed?'

Eva was getting vexatious. I could see it.

'It's a simple request, will you please make up my sheets? The bed's been taken away.'

And sure enough it had. In the middle of the carpet in her small room was a dusty oblong shape. It was the shadow of where her bed had been – a bit like the outline of a murder victim – and in the middle of that lay the bed linen and blankets. I had to make her bed up under strict supervision: the sheets were to be folded into a basic origami with just one blanket on top. I didn't ask about her bedtime ritual. I didn't want to know because I had the nagging feeling that there would be enough opportunity to find out more in the coming days. Eva, I had decided, was not only bitter: she was a complete head-case.

CARABINIERI

I woke up to fabulous sunshine. Even the miserable hotel looked better in it. It was a chance for another fab fashion moment. I put on my groovy Mao Tse-tung vest, last night's linen shorts and crippling Indian flip-flops in preparation for the next leg of the journey. I found the invalid in her deconstructed bedroom. It was looking more like a student doss-house than a boudoir, and she was welcome to it. I gathered her luggage, staggered downstairs like a deranged shopaholic and made for the station while she settled the bill. A porter rescued me. I was a millisecond away from falling into a Merchant Ivory moment. It was to be Edwardian travel arrangements and me playing the fragile English gent abroad. I would be thrown on the mercy of the horny-handed Italian machismo-man. I could see myself in a dove grey suit with a high lapel and white gloves. I was virginal yet seething with repressed desire. ***Eva awareness***: she needed rescuing too. Time to abandon daydream and see to the infirm. We were getting more looks.

Buying the tickets was one thing, boarding the train was another. Moustachioed porterman kindly helped with the bags and I dealt resentfully with Eva. The train was mobbed and I pushed her into a compartment. I found her a seat with half a doz of Sicily's finest: hirsute, excitable, animated farmers all dressed in suits and on their way to a wedding. Well, why else would a farmer wear a suit? They were evidently enjoying themselves. She, apparently, was not. The miserable woman could vibe out the host country but she wasn't going to fuck up on my amusement. I sat on the juicer in the corridor, soaking up the sun and watching the wonderful baked countryside disappear. The trip had nothing to do with companionship, thank fuck. She could do her own thing, and I was definitely going to do mine. I stayed in the corridor chatting to a long-haired Ozzy backpacker called Neil for the three hours it took to get to Messina. He gave me a contact number in London, which I stored optimistically in the *fux* section.

Eva and I were the only people to get off; it was like the other passengers had a tacit understanding that this was a place to miss out on. The train moved on and left us on the platform, there were no porters, the station was deserted. I gathered up the luggage and headed towards an exit, hoping for signs to the harbour, which was where we were to get a boat.

It was very hot and Eva was still dressed for her split journey. The Benidorm half was doing just fine but her lower extremities, still packaged up for an oncoming polar winter, looked like they – rather than cancer – might just do her in. We were standing near the station, enveloped in dust, heat and truculence. We were lost, not that Eva would admit to it. Yeah, yeah, she'd been there before, she'd told me a dozen times, but there was no way she knew where she was going now.

'Ah, I think I recognise this, Jake.'

'Wouldn't it be better to ask for directions rather than scab around in the heat?'

She glared at me. 'I've been here before, you know.'

'So you keep saying, Eva.'

'I have.'

'As a Red Indian squaw in a previous existence perhaps, but not bloody recently. I'm going to ask someone.' I turned to head back towards the station (after having a queeny hissy-fit and dumping all the luggage on the pavement) and was promptly ambushed by a very ancient and very little old man. I reckoned my pheromones were losing something in their translation. Where were all the sweaty Italian stallions with hard gangster bodies oozing with latent homosexuality? Where were the bruised young men with bee-stung lips, gagging for a shag with a fruit on vacation? I mean, this was southern Italy, for fuck's sake. There had to be a closet somewhere stuffed full of illicit naughtiness. I could dream on. And what did this old sod want? He threw his arms up into the air, started babbling, then kissed me. He was very pleased to see me. In the circumstances I was glad that anyone was. After much incomprehension and pantomime gesture I got the drift that it wasn't so much me but more my Mao singlet that had got him going. It was a singular and puzzling disappointment. As he did more big attitude hand-waving and talking the lira dropped: I realised that he was an old-school Commie who thought that I must be a young comrade, a political idealist, one of Them. He'd got it wrong: I just liked the vest.

'What's Italian for fashion, Eva? Mao Tse-tung Armani, *vestino* Gucci, *singletti* Versace, darling. It's very now.'

I'd got a fan. Eva looked like she could wrap herself inside out with frustration and evidently hated the old man as well as me.

'When you've quite finished, Jake, we have a boat to find.'

'Eva, there was me thinking you knew exactly where you were going. I think Lenin here will help. *Scusa*, Aliscafi?'

'*Si, si*, Aliscafi, *non c'è problema*.'

Lenin was only too pleased to help his new red friend find his way to the port and the boat. The sourpuss Eva couldn't help herself looking momentarily content at the prospect of getting to where she wanted to be. We neared the harbour.

Our progress might politely have been called stately – Eva and Lenin were incapable of anything other than a crawl – but it was loud. Lenin made a surprising amount of noise for a geriatric, yelling over to his less able-bodied party-member mates who seemed to populate every café and street corner. We were at the front of the heavy artillery, striding ahead of the massed ranks of foot soldiers, and in advance of the nuclear arsenal. Red Square had never looked so good and we had never been so conspicuous: two invalids and a queen reeling past the Politburo.

We got to the docks and I met the *carabinieri* for the first time, or maybe it was they who met me. ***Reality check eight***: these guys are reconstituted Nazis, souped-up cops in sexy uniforms with a spiteful attitude. They were going to fuck with me. In broken English they wanted to know who I was, where I was going, was I a Communist, who was she, what did I want around here? I toyed with replying, in decimated Italian, that I was the supreme leader of a pink socialist movement, headed for my new luxury villa with my very own handmaiden in tow and was expecting to bugger all the shepherds on the island. However as this was my first run-in with the cretins, I sensibly didn't. But by this stage I was in vacation mode. I didn't need any shit from wannabe Rambos in Peasantville. I was ready for battle as only a homo-on-holiday can be and deftly sorted out the pig problem with blind indifference. My prehistoric Communist admirer cheered me as I turned away from the Gestapo. I went to the office, picked up two tickets for the Aliscafi, waved goodbye to my political playmate, scooped up the luggage, with Eva in tow, and went to board the boat.

'No.'

'*Scusa*, *doway* tickets for the boat, *perfervori*.'

'No.'

'I've got two frigging tickets for the boat, big boy, what's your problem?'

The ticket collector was having none of it. Even though the boat was half full there was no way he was letting Eva or me on board. I couldn't figure out if he was a job'sworth, a dickhead, in cahoots with the *carabinieri*, or simply antagonised by my shirt. I put it down to the latter. We had to wait for another boat that was due in two hours' time. I was in an invincible, if slightly battered, mood and nothing was going to get me down; heck, I was going to enjoy myself whatever happened and a couple of loons with port authority were not going to make an impression. We decamped to a café.

'Jake, why do you have to create trouble wherever you go?'

'What do you mean?'

'Well, if you hadn't decided to wear politically sensitive clothing then perhaps we'd be on the boat now. This delay is all your fault.'

'Eva, I'm wearing a frigging vest that I bought in Camden market because I liked the image. I'm hardly on a subversive mission to destabilise the political topography of Italy.'

My momentary triumph of locating the harbour was forgotten.

'This whole problem is down to you, Jake. Just look at you.'

She riled me because, secretly, I knew she had a point. On my last trip away – when I was in Paris – I'd been stopped at Immigration for wearing the Tom of Finland T-shirt. I'd put that incident down to a Parisian taste bypass, but I'd known I was wrong.

'I'm sorry, but this is the way I dress, like it or lump it. How was I to know that a vest would cause anarchy at a ticket office? Funnily enough, it's not something I consider before making a trip.'

We sat in the café. I ordered a small carafe of white wine and dared Eva to say anything. She didn't. After our little run-in with the cops and the ticket inspector, and our dwarfish spat, the vibe levels gradually subsided. I began to chill for the first time since leaving London. I think even Eva did because there were moments when her stony face softened.

* * *

It was time to get the Aliscafi. We got on with no probs this time and headed out towards Vulcano. I was excited now. We sat outside above the motors at the back of the surprisingly flashy craft. It was loud and wet as the spray from the boat shot up and covered us. It was cool, and it was fast. It was just the type of thing Judith Chalmers might enjoy. Dressed in a sarong and brightly coloured T-shirt she'd lean back and pout towards the camera with her middle-aged take on girlish frivolity. I could see her orange cleavage heave with the swell and her iced-pink lippy extolling the wonderment of cruising the islands. *Wish You Were Here?* You bet. Yep, we were on holiday now.

VULCANO

A faint smell of sulphur had been detectable in the air for quite some time, but when we disembarked the stench was overwhelming. This wasn't some minor pong or an old lady's lapse: it was a full-on gut-rotting vapour. The island smelt ill and looked pre-Cambrian. It was an unusual holiday destination. ***Reality check nine***: the smell was inescapable. It was as if half a dozen incontinents had been put on an egg-only diet for a week. Mind-blowing. The harbour was denuded and poor-looking. There was one store that tried vainly to sell crap to the few tourists who remained at the end of the season, and a couple of other buildings that were crumbling and looked unused. It was the type of place that had been something once, but not any more. It was one part aquatic spaghetti-western to two parts cheap chemistry set. Our baggage had piled up on the quayside. Eva, thankfully, had had the foresight to book ahead and what appeared to be the only car on the prehistoric isle had come to greet us. It was acrid, acid and arid. We'd arrived.

The car pulled away from the port and drove a shortish distance past a ruined house and a landscape that looked as if it were the result of an industrial accident. There was yellow earth and black earth; it looked sterile and inert. The vegetation was dying and dust covered everything. It owed more to the Malcolm Forbes School of Chemical Engineering (Bhopal Branch) than it did to a Mediterranean sunshine resort. We drove past muddy ponds and on towards the Casa Becci.

The hotel was conceived in a Moorish manner that had missed, style-wise, big-time. The reception area was cool and airy, but very dark. There was lots of wood, that bad-good-taste wood that has had its corners knocked off and filed down to give it a regular antique finish. It was not unlike the type of ye olde worlde crap that you find in rubbishy pubs. Everything that could have been given a false provenance had been. All that was missing were several suits of armour. Naff roof beams, which had also been distressed, held up the high ceiling; embossed leather, the odd shield and huge lumpy bits of furniture were everywhere. I sat in one of the very solid chairs, got out my Filofax and added the hotel number. ***Interior décor awareness***: Casa Becci reception was Spanish-Inquisition luxe.

Eva and I were led through the hotel, past a large patio, where a late lunch was still being cleared, past other Euro-trash (I couldn't get a grip on who was there in the talent department), and on to our rooms, which were housed in what looked like a large bungalow to the side of the main hotel. The extension was a dodgy Dallas of a place: a bit Southfork meets Vulcano. It wouldn't have been a surprise to find the members of the Oil Barons' Ball Committee sipping margaritas, chomping on cigars and plotting another takeover – I was convinced I'd already caught a glimpse of Bobby and Sue Ellen. What the fuck? There was sand, sea and sun, wasn't there? ***Factor eight awareness***: get out the Lycra swim trunks – cut ludicrously high to make my legs look three inches longer – and get the bod straight into the surf. Bliss, total fabulous bliss. Somehow it didn't smell as much in this neck of the woods.

I saw Eva come out of her room and sit in the shade; she gave a little wave. Was that a genuine salutation or was it a pathetic little wave designed to generate guilt? Presumably the latter. She looked miserable.

I walked up to her. 'Eva, you're still wearing those crazy leggings. Are you preparing for a cold snap or do you think the thermals could come off now?'

'I have to wear them.'

'I don't think so. I'll be back in a min.'

Decision time: do I pull something out of my bag for Eva to put on or don't I? I don't. I'd buy her something instead. I nipped back to the harbour shop, honed my fashion radar and located a couple of enormous white silk scarves with silver thread running through them. They were massive Indian chiffon jobs. I headed back to the hotel. 'Here, something a bit cooler to wear.'

'What are they?' Eva was peering at them suspiciously.

'Well, what do you think they are? Couture curtains? They're a couple of light scarves that might possibly feel better to wear than thick woollens. In case you hadn't noticed, it's way up in the thirties and wearing a polar fleece isn't a hip idea. Besides, those trousers make your bump look even bigger.'

They certainly did: her extension looked enormous under

her elasticated-waist wool pants. She didn't say anything and averted her gaze from the scarves to her navel. It was the first time that I'd mentioned her bizarre gut and I felt contrite for having done so. But it was true: her hump did look big, it was massive. Eva remained in the shade and the scarves stayed on the table. I went back into the sea: I'd made it my mission to cruise anyone who looked remotely tasty. I'd mutated into a basking shark.

There was no more travelling. I was already beginning to get colour and there was time to relax, provided it was away from Eva. I decided that I needed to establish independence quickly and develop my own enterprises if this trip was going to work. She might be unwell, but we didn't need to be with each other at every minute. The prospects didn't look good, though: escape routes and distractions appeared to be scarce.

The scarves were worn on the first night of the first real day of our holiday: Eva had wrapped one around her waist and draped the other round her neck. She looked good, but didn't say anything about them. Dinner was served outside on the patio; the set-up looked a bit dull. There were a few Italian families spread out at different tables, all dressed for the occasion in tasteless comfy clothes – the men looked like slack-ridden poofs and the women had Stepford gazes. It felt a bit too nice and far too well-mannered – even the kids spoke with hushed voices – and the likelihood of discovering a shag was increasingly remote. The food was pretty yummy, though. There was fresh seafood with a scrummy tomato and basil sauce, and fresh pasta, delish salad and, thankfully, lots of white wine. I assumed Eva was beginning to enjoy herself as she didn't comment on my consumption of *vino*. She said nothing about the ciggies either. We were having a pleasant time, given that we didn't like each other.

'Would you like to come for a little walk with me after dinner, Jake?'

'Well, why not? That would be lovely. Where do you fancy going?'

'Just anywhere.'

The sky and sea were quite black. Another island in the distance – Lipari – was only discernible because of a few tiny lights winking at us. We walked down on to the sand away from the restaurant behind us.

'It's better if I can walk at this time of night, Jake.'

'Why? Because it's cooler?'

'No, because no one can see me when it's dark.'

I felt a bit sorry for her, not that she'd have been overjoyed to be the focus of my pity. 'Well, I hope you don't become nocturnal on me because this place ain't geared up for it. You can't hide all day,' I said.

She didn't answer. There was no one around and it felt great – warmth and sand always does. I was enjoying hanging out in the night-time air. We sat down at the water's edge and peered into the night. Above Lipari fireworks exploded. Massive Disneyesque dandelion heads powered into the sky and reflected in the still sea.

'Why do they have to be so vulgar?'

'What do you mean, Eva?'

'It's so peaceful here without those fireworks. Don't you think they're crude? So . . . middle class?'

Euphoria was out: it looked as if even the simplest pleasure had no chance of surviving around her.

'No, not really, I think they look fab. I can't believe you don't.'

She was the type of woman who thought ostentation coarse and vulgar, something that she most definitely wasn't. Anal, yes, ostentatious, never.

'Where do you live, Jake?'

'Gospel Oak. What about you?'

'I have a house in Belsize Park.'

We were near neighbours. Eva went on to describe her place. She lived in one of those huge stucco-fronted jobs; massive, with enormous windows that let in so much light the place seemed even bigger. It didn't sound so much a home as a tribal compound.

'It's too big for just one so I've a couple of friends who live there too. You met them at the airport.'

I fished to see if lookout man was anything more than just a pal, and Eva scowled at me. She was quite good at withering glances. Her eyes were so exceptionally blue they might have belonged to a Pantone card. It seemed possible that she could fix you with them and, like a laser, singe you from the other side of a room. She had that confident, careful manner, which is only achieved with a Coutts Bank account and a platinum Amex; she was sloppy-mid-European luxe. There was nothing flashy about her, just luxurious understatement – she was a bit like her house, bourgeois German ex-hippie to the tiles. I could imagine her living room: there'd be a large, depressing piece of existential artwork hung on a vast white wall. A cunningly positioned post-modern Scandinavian chair in bleached maple would be wittily juxtaposed with an ethnic rug, dried flowers and fruit. Perhaps a simple lingam would be resplendent on the mantelpiece. All a bit *feng shui* before its time. Too Chinese-Germanic up its own butt*shui*.

'Jake, are you falling asleep?'

I came to.

'C'mon, neighbour, it's been a very long day – I need to rest. Will you help me sort out the bed again?'

We got to the rooms and I farted around with her sheets once more. She still wasn't using a bed.

'By the way, Jake, thank you for the scarves. I do like them.'

A GROPE IN THE DARK

Brekky. Eva found me lounging on one of the big wicker chairs on the veranda wearing what I thought passed off rather successfully as full Arab sheikh drag.

'You look, er, colourful today, Jake. Is this the latest in beachwear?'

'It's my take on Saudi, d'yer like it?'

I hadn't got Eva's juicer working yet so I thought I'd check out the locally squashed produce. It was very good. I was swigging at a fresh orange juice, which I'd polluted with plenty of vodka, and she joined me for one of her infusions and some fruit.

'Is that any good, Jake?'

'What?'

'The juice.'

'It's delicious.'

Eva's bony hand stretched out and took my glass for a slurp. 'That's disgusting. What's wrong with it?'

'Nothing.'

'Don't try to kid me! What have you done to it? There must be half a bottle of alcohol in that shit. Didn't I tell you I want purity around me, not a branch of Alcoholics Anonymous?'

'And I think I told you I'm the baggage-handler. It *is* pure anyway. It's Stoly.'

Eva went back to her healthy drink and I stayed with mine.

'Jake, did you notice what the rates are in your room?'

'No, was I supposed to?'

'That would be the normal thing to do, or are you above that Jake?'

Eva was budgeting and I didn't want anything to do with it. I didn't want any fiscal crap. I didn't have any money and it wasn't part of the deal. 'If you're so worried about them why don't you check at Reception? It's obviously expensive – I mean, don't you know what this place costs?'

'This is what you should be doing, Jake. This is what I employ you for,' Eva snapped.

'Let's get this straight, Eva. You're not employing me, Richard sent me along, remember? If you're unhappy with the hotel, then sort it out. I mean, what's the big deal? Richard's paying for me anyway.'

There was a long silence; I could see her thinking.

'No, he isn't, Jake, I am.'

What the fuck? I knew I wasn't her ideal travelling companion, but then she wasn't mine. I was hardly responsible for the travel plans; I hadn't booked the hotel and I wasn't paying for it either. I concentrated on topping up the juice with another super-dose of vodders and tried vainly to ease the situation. 'It's not as if we're staying here for ever. We'll be gone in a couple more days.'

But Eva had already vanished to Reception. She returned

with an equally eaten-up look and sat down with her offensive Japanese tea. It was the beginning of another uncomfortable truce. I was uneasy: I needed to lighten the atmosphere. 'Why don't we go to the mud pools today?'

She froze me out.

'Look, we've travelled half-way over Europe to get here, why don't we go for a paddle?'

'No.'

She wasn't going to budge.

'So, what do you want to do? Hang out in a darkened bedroom looking at your origami bed all day, doing nothing?'

Eva pursed her face in another of her extraordinary grimaces.

'Fuck it, Eva, Vulcano is too dull to do nothing on. Let's do something, for God's sake.'

She conceded. We'd go for a walk. Well, a shuffle.

We started back towards the harbour. The road split and, instead of reaching the port, we headed to the left behind a huge craggy mound that smelt like those loose eggy farts had done their best again. We were within a stink-bomb's whiff of unconsciousness. Around the outcrop was a large ship, a huge umbilical cord stretched from its belly to the shore, but instead of taking nourishment the vast baby was emptying its insides, a fresh-water delivery for the island to drink. We headed away, still in our slow-mo-action-replay mode in contrast to everybody else's normal pace. Folks were striding past, having a surreptitious look then hurrying on. We were attracting attention again. There weren't exactly dozens of people taking a sneaky look at breakneck pedestrian speeds, but the few who did were noticeable.

Eva decided to let me in a little more on the story of her cancer as we trudged through the crumbling yellow and black broken earth. 'This is something I'm going to kill, Jake, it's not going to get me.'

She was hissing rather than talking; she sounded like a flattening tyre.

'I'm strong, my mind is strong, and I'm going to finish the cancer off. I can do it, you know. I'm nearly there.'

She told me how she visualised the disease. 'It's like it's not really a part of me, Jake. It belongs elsewhere. I suppose what I hate the most is the way it's changed me. I still can't understand how I've inherited a body that belongs to someone else.'

I could see that she had been a handsome woman before her body had readjusted itself into something alien. She was well and truly fucked now. Her fine hair was long and there was a lot of it. Her upper torso was skeletal – her breasts looked like empty purses with small nipple clasps – while her stomach was distended and looked as if it might burst under the pressure. Her legs were positively elephantine. Every movement she made hurt and every hurt was an effort. We kept getting looks.

'Why do they keep looking? Do they know I have cancer?'

'Hardly. Just look at the two of us – wouldn't you look?'

'What do you mean?'

'You're hardly promenading with Arnie Schwarzenegger, now, are you?'

I was billowing along the dirt tracks wearing just the outer layer of my Saudi-prince-does-Frisco get-up – an absurd silk organza coat – my skimpy trunks and a funky vest. Eva hobbled along with her new scarves wrapped around her bloated tummy and a huge blue shirt. The two of us had to stop every few paces for Eva to regain her breath; the patient was puffing and the poof was trying to be patient. The more she thought people were watching, the more convoluted her theories became.

'No, you're right, this isn't about my cancer. This is about body fascism.'

'I beg your pardon?'

'Yes, this is all about the politics of the body, the sexuality of form.'

'Eva, I think you've lost it.'

'No, I can see it. It's fine for an old man to have a stomach that dangles over his waistband, but for a woman it is taboo. No?'

'No, darling, believe me, it is not OK. You're talking to a faggot, for Chrissakes, someone who worships at the shrine of Adolf when it comes to body fascism. It's a capital offence for anyone to have excess flesh, regardless of sex.'

'I didn't think it was like that here.'

'Don't you believe it, Eva. We're getting looks because people think we're freaks. I've seen it before a thousand times. They think we're an odd couple.'

Our shuffle took us back via the mud pools – there were a few people in them – then slowly on to the Casa Becci.

Back at base, we were greeted with the news that the hotel was closing early – it would be open only for another two days. I wondered whether or not Eva's chat about the prices had prompted this: perhaps the management had decided that for the sake of a few extra lire it was easier to get shot of her than stay open. It didn't really matter: Vulcano, like everything else, was coming to the end of its season.

We'd missed lunch, not that either of us needed it. Eva went to ask about alternative accommodation and I went to work on my tan, hanging out on the beach but not feeling quite comfortable. Eva was omnipresent. Dinner was on the veranda overlooking the ocean, and I was getting a distinct vibe from the waiter who was serving us. He was Gio's *Doppelgänger*; one could only pray that he was cursed with the same handicap. There were a lot of smiles from my new friend and much eye-contact; I was feeling thoroughly at home, horny, and gagging for a postprandial porking. Eva moseyed off to her Zen-inspired sleeping quarters, and I hung around the veranda for another drink and, perhaps, a little after-hours' activity with my latest buddy. All the nice Italian families had left; it was just me enjoying the atmosphere.

'Can I have another drink, please?'

'Of course. You not with your friend this evening?'

'Nope, she's gone to bed. I'm Jake, by the way.'

'I know. Alessandro. So you're by yourself this evening. You not lonely?'

'I'll survive. Why? Do you want to keep me company?'

'Sure. I finish work now. What you like to do? Maybe we go for a constitutional?'

What was this guy like? Constitutional? He must have learnt his English in the 1900s. Fuck it, all I'd got to do so far was perambulate so what was to stop me from noctambulating too?

'Yeah, let's. Where to?'

'I show you around, Jake, you'll like it.'

We headed off together. Alessandro was still wearing his waiter's outfit and plastic name badge. Maybe his mum had been a glamour model because he'd inherited all the requisite characteristics of a page-three girl. He was the type of guy who verged on petulance; he was sultry and pouting, sexy yet demanding. That didn't make him undesirable, far from it. His eyes were strange almond slits that looked shifty and he'd got a great body. Alessandro excited me. We mooched to the top of a hill and saw the beginnings of a smallish town down below. It didn't look very alive at eleven thirty on a Wednesday night, but there again nothing was feeling very alive. We skirted back towards the mud pools.

'What you do in London, Jake?'

I started the designer spiel. It was a conversation that was almost identical to the one I'd had with Gio in the sauna.

'You have a nice house?'

'Yeah, it's kinda big. It's in Belsize Park. I've done it in a minimalist way – I've got a lot of artwork that goes really neatly with my Scandinavian furniture. It's great.'

Reality check ten: I had described Eva's place – it suited the imaginary professional status. I felt like a prat. Why was I bullshitting and trying to overimpress this guy with a second-hand description of somebody else's place? I was being an arsehole and hastily tried to backtrack, which didn't work because Alessandro had now got it firmly stuck in his head that I was at least on a par with Armani.

'You must be very important.'

'I'm not, really. I just made what I do sound exciting. My job is very ordinary, it's nothing.'

Alessandro had other ideas: he was looking very sparkly of eye.

'Maybe I come and stay with you in London.'

'I don't think so, babes.'

'Yes, it would be good. I love London. I love you.'

I'd fucked up again. I'd stoked this bloke up into a flurry of expectation. I'd pushed his opportunity button and he was priming himself for a new life with a sugar-daddy.

'Darling, hate to disappoint, but I'm broke. I can barely look after myself let alone support you.'

'It's OK, I look after you in your house.'

'Al, I really don't need an Italian-lady-boy-that-does.'

I'd gone and got myself a mummy's boy looking for a sugar-shag, a wimp looking for a chance.

'You know, the season finishes soon, I can come to London then, Jake.'

All my protestations of normalness were dismissed as nothing more than false modesty: Al could see an opportunity and he was going for it. Everyone was looking for opportunity, Eva, Al, me. We were all looking to escape from something and all of us were ready to take whatever came our respective ways.

'Jake, I like your costume, let me see . . .'

We were sitting by one of the rank ponds and Alessandro was getting all frisky and snog-oriented. We pulled off each other's garb and kicked up a cloud of dust punctuated by legs and arms, like cartoon characters having a scrap. It was fun, although the *doppel*'s *gänger* was nowhere near as miraculous as Gio's – just goes to show you can't have everything, huh? We managed to get sand in all the wrong places and to attract the attention of somebody who walked by at a crucial stage in the proceedings. We'd started so we had to finish, distant spectator or not. I decided Alessandro was a sweetie and we slunk back to the hotel together.

'Jake, perhaps we meet up again tomorrow night?'

'Yeah, I'd love to, let's talk in the morning. Goodnight.'

I was up before Eva again, but this time I'd decided on an outfit that was a little more informal – my rent-boy shorts (old jeans sawn off so high they were barely decent) and a tight white T. Alessandro was doing the morning shift and was busy with the other guests. Eva joined me just as he came bounding over with an over-exuberance of post-last-night attentiveness.

'How are you both this sunny morning? A good night's sleep?'

I feigned coolness. 'Fine, thank you Al. Could you get me some juice, please?'

Eva looked on with raised eyebrows. She actually looked quite *smutty*, which I'd hardly expected. 'So, were you busy last night, Jake?'

'Mmm?'

'I think you were, you sex-crazed alcoholic you.'

I got the feeling she was being affectionate with me. She was having her own little joke. I said nothing and made out that I was admiring the horizon.

'Eva, shall we check out those ponds today?'

'No, not yet.'

Another refusal at the second fence.

'I need to find a new place for us to stay. Somewhere cheaper. And when will we get fruit for that bloody juice machine, Jake?'

We decided on another of our slow-mo transits through the decimated landscape to hunt for a supply of carrots. I took Eva to the town I'd seen the previous night and located the local fruit 'n' veg shop. It looked as if it hadn't had a dusting since sometime before Vulcano's volcano last erupted – the early 1890s. Among all the crates of not-so-fresh-looking veg were the carrots. We'd struck tuberous gold. Next stop was a villa that had been recommended by the hotel. We veered away from the settlement and along the lane. Just up from what had become a dirt track was the house, covered in bougainvillaea and very pretty. It didn't take long to decide on it as the ideal refuge.

'I have to take this for a week, Jake, and I want you to stay the extra days, OK?'

Well, that was just tickety-boo: I needed no excuse to avoid work for another seven days. I was sure Richard would understand, because I was doing his friend such a big favour. And if he didn't, who cared? We went back to the hotel to settle up and pack our bags.

I said goodbye to Alessandro, who looked a little antsy. 'Where are you going? Are you going back?'

'I'm not leaving the island, just moving into a villa up the hill. I'll see you around.'

The hotel lent us their car and we moved into our new home. It was pretty basic. You walked straight into a small kitchen at the side of the house and then into a living room. At the back were two bedrooms, sparse but comfy. I took the left-hand room and Eva decided to create her own suite. 'I will use the bedroom as a dressing room, and this is where I sleep.' She had staked her claim to the living room. She could have it.

We began to reassemble our crap in our respective territories and generally nested. I cranked up the juicer and shoved through the first couple of pounds of carrots.

'Are you going to have a glass as well, Jake?'

The drink looked fine, but I didn't think so: there was only so much good living I could take. 'Perhaps we could buy tomatoes next time and make Bloody Marys?'

Eva ignored me.

Suppertime, and I was starving. We went back into the not-tropolis and found a pizzeria a little further down the road from the greengrocer's. It was optimistically aimed at the tourist trade but was empty except for another guy sitting opposite.

Even Eva was surprised at the deathliness of the place. 'Jake, shall we ask that chap to join us?'

This was unexpected progress on the sociability front.

'Sure, let's be friendly, I'll ask him. Excuse me. Hello? Would you like to join us?'

The blond looked a little taken aback. 'No, it's OK. Thank you.'

'C'mon, it's dumb you eating by yourself. Join us, go on.'

A little persuasion did the trick and he pulled up his chair. 'Thanks, my name's Stefan, it's nice to meet you. It's nice to meet anyone here – this place is so dead. Are you on holiday too?'

Stefan was a babe, a tall Swiss babe on hols from his shop job. He was on the island to get dirty – for poofy beauty treatments rather than for health reasons. He was good company. So was Eva. She was genuinely pleasant for the first time, making cryptic remarks about Alessandro and even having a glass of wine. I guess we were finding our own space, and now that we had defined boundaries we were relaxing in each other's company. Strangely we – or, more to the point, I – still got weird vibes and an undertone of hostility from the locals. It bugged Eva, but I didn't give a toss: we were freaks, marked people, and I was used to it.

'Eva, Jake, I'm off now. Thanks for this evening. I was beginning to think I was the only person on this island. Shall we have dinner together again? How about tomorrow?'

'Yeah, we'll look out for you.'

We said goodnight to Stefan and made our way home in the dark surrounded by cacti and aloe, only to be stopped by the *carabinieri*.

'What you do here? Who are you? Where you go? What you do on Vulcano?'

I was getting v. pissed off. 'You know exactly who we are. We've been the island's only source of amusement for the past few days. You don't mean to say you've missed out on the fun?'

The cop ignored me. 'I want to know why you here.'

'I'm on frigging holiday.'

Eva pushed me away before I made a scene, calmed me

down, dealt with the police and pointed me in the direction of the villa.

'Oh, Jake, just one thing, don't use the bathroom. Use the hose outside, please.'

'What?'

'We'll talk about this tomorrow, but for now go outside. Please help me with my bed – get this furniture out of the way, over there, that's it. Goodnight.'

Eva had gone obsessional on me. I had guessed it would only be a matter of time. ***Personal hygiene awareness***: I had been partially banned from using the bathroom in the villa. It was OK for me to crap and pee, provided I aimed properly, and fine to shave, but not OK for me to wash, brush my teeth or bathe. If I wanted to shower I had to use the hosepipe in the back garden or scrub myself discreetly in the sea. What was going on in her head? I was fucked if I was going to find out. It was easier to play along with her neurosis than understand it.

Eva's bedmaking was another fixation. The furniture in the living room, not that there was much, had been pushed back to the walls leaving a big space in the middle of the floor. Every night, in the centre of the room, I would lay out a blanket folded in two then place the precious sheet on top. It was vital to the process that the sheet was the right way up, with that extra inch of hem that runs along the top edge at the head of the bed.

'Jake. Do this again. I can't sleep like that, it's not right.'

'What difference does it make?'

'It's the way it's got to be done. I don't have to explain everything to you, do I? It has to be perfect.'

If the sheet was reversed or, worse, at a right angle to true, the whole exacting routine had to be started again from the beginning. The top sheet was then folded neatly in two with the gap on the right, the top corner then being folded down forty-five degrees leaving space for a pillow with another blanket placed loosely on top of the precision-pleated ply. It was as if any variation would prove dangerous. Each night Eva inspected the bed, like a dog turning round in its basket, and only then was it safe for her to get into it.

BABY-TALK

Alessandro made it his mission to trace us to the villa. It didn't take much initiative.

'Oh, *ciao*, Jake,' like it was a surprise, 'it's good to see you. What are you doing today?'

I was doing bugger all: Eva had decided to take a kip and I was itching for a diversion. I'd just got one. 'Nothing, Al, do you fancy another walk?'

I was answered with a huge grin, and we loped off the track that led towards the beach and headed up on to the scraggy hillside.

'We have to be careful. No one must see.'

'Relax, Al, who's interested anyway?'

'There was talk at the hotel. Someone saw us the other night.'

I didn't think it could be possible to keep anything secret around here, especially information concerning an assignation beside a dirty pond. But, then, what did I care? We scrambled up through a copse and climbed behind a large rock. I love *al fresco* bonks, even if they're a little perilous.

'What the fuck are you trying to do, Al?'

'I think maybe you like.'

'Carry on thinking, but without a condom nothing will be happening in that department. Haven't you heard of safe sex?'

'Go on, it's nature.'

'Get stuffed, Al, it's suicide.'

Hazardous sex is fine, provided the worst that can happen is falling down the hillside, but unprotected sex has always been a complete no-no. We got on with something a little more creative instead.

'I see you later tonight?'

'I don't know, Al. It depends on what Eva fancies. I mean, I don't know if we're going out for dinner or what. I'll keep an eye out for you.'

I got back to the villa looking a little flushed – from the mountaineering rather than the shag.

Eva was sitting in a scrap of garden beneath the bougainvillaea. 'Where were you? I've been sitting here by myself for ages.'

'I've been for a walk. Is that OK or do I need permission?'

'It would be nice if you could let me know if you're going to vanish for the morning.'

'Eva, I've been for a walk, what's your problem now?'

She was annoyed, but none the wiser. She didn't know that I'd been on an erotic excursion, which was a good job as she was looking poisonous. When she got tight like this I felt trapped; I needed to escape. Alessandro suddenly appeared by the garden gate.

'What's he doing here, Jake?'

'How should I know? Hi, Alessandro!'

I walked down to greet him, confused as to why he should have popped back up again so swiftly. 'What are you doing here?' I asked.

'I want to see you.'

I was being stalked. 'We just have seen each other – intimately.'

Alessandro was doing his hurt-Bambi look and I was having difficulty trying to understand his fixation. What the fuck was he about?

'I think that we spend the day together, Jake. We could go to the beach.'

'It's not possible, Al.'

'But I like.'

'I'm sure you do, but you'll have to sod off. I've got to hang out with Eva.'

Saying no to Alessandro was like disciplining a muppet. I felt a bit guilty – I didn't want to def the guy out completely.

'Look, do you fancy meeting me by the ponds again at midnight?'

That was an affirmative. He walked off happy and I felt good. I needed Al like he thought he needed me.

'What's going on between you and that boy, Jake? Have you been with him all morning?'

'Eva, what is it with you? So what if I have?'

'I want to know, that's all.'

'There's nothing to know. He's fond of me and I quite like him, that's all.'

Eva went into the gloomy room to lie on her fanatical-far-out futon with her scrotal stole wrapped snugly around her shoulders. 'Jake, I'm hungry. Why don't you go to the market at the harbour and see if you can get some fish?'

'Is there one?'

'What?'

'Market. Is there one?'

'Well, why don't you use your eyes and go and see?'

There was. It wasn't really a market, more of a canvas booth by the crumbly buildings and the knackered tourist shop. A couple of guys were sitting in the shade beside an enormous pile of baby squid. They looked tasty.

'Do you have anything else?'

They looked at me as if I were a moron and pointed towards the squid with a shrug. I got the message and bought half a kilo, then nipped into the veg shop, got carrots and a hutch-worth of salad, located a deli and bought ham. I could feel the sun burn through my shirt as I walked back to the villa. I was sweating; and my clothes were sticking to me. The dust was wafting up behind me as I trudged with another two hundred POWs past the Japanese guards. It was tough building a bridge over the River Kwai. We kept in step as the platoon neared the camp. Barbed wire ran between the lookout towers, and I didn't know if I could make it. Just another few paces. Water, water. As spokesman for the rest of the men it was my responsibility to see the camp commandant. I neared the gatehouse and prepared myself for a dressing down. I entered the office and found Eva, who was still in an uncertain mood and sitting in the dark.

'Eva, if you want me to cook all this I'm happy to, but

I'll need adult supervision if you expect me to gut these creatures.'

She lumbered over to the sink and, with Germanic precision, nipped out the ink sac, pulled out the pesky blade that sits inside the beastie and generally cleaned it up. She made it look so easy. By the time I'd finished the rest, the kitchen had become a piscine abattoir with squid juice everywhere. It was kinda macabre. Inky fingerprints were all over the draining-board, on the walls and spattered on the door. Great smears of the black, bloody, butchery liquid had made themselves a focal point on my forehead and shirt. The mess was an abstract history of my recent movements: like a dot-to-dot puzzle in a kiddies' comic. The squid grilled gloriously, as did the crispy pancetta. I served up the fab-a-mondo concoction with a yummy salad on the side. I was more than pleased with my culinary skills. I felt like a six-year-old coming home with schoolwork that had been given a gold star by teacher and pride of place on the fridge door. There's something really satisfying about cooking. I love it, even if the kitchen does look as if a horror movie has been condensed into twenty minutes of frenzied action over the stove.

I made more juice, enjoyed more afternoon heat, got into more routine and embraced domesticity for the first time in my life. Washing-up had never been a strong point but I was rather enjoying it. Each day had gradually taken on a regularity punctuated by the juicing of carrots, swimming, the folding of linen, the snicking outside for fags and washes, with shuffled walks and the anticipated probings with Al thrown in for good measure.

We went for yet another ambulation. This time it was Eva's turn for excitement. Yes, wow, she could go into the veg shop for the buy-of-the-day, the purchase of a kilo of rootlets. I was watching an ex-hippie trying to kill a tumour with a tuber. If I'm honest I was getting a little bored. I was thinking about Alessandro: what does a waiter do in a hotel that has just closed down for the season? Maybe they were secretly open and just wanted to get rid of the gangrenous German and the peroxide poof. I fantasised on. I wondered what Gio was up to; perhaps he was working his carnal charm on somebody else. ***Reality check eleven***: what the fuck was Eva doing? Just how long does it take to buy root vegetables? She came out into the bright sunshine with two elderly women, the three of them laughing and talking in German.

'Jake, this is Gertrude *und* this is Gretel.'

'Hi.'

'They are staying at the other hotel, the Garden Hotel.'

That was news to me: I'd thought that Vulcano was barely able to support one let alone two hostelries. After all, it was virtually a one-car town.

'Gertrude has a daughter Karin who works there.'

Gertrude and Gretel were identical twins, lined and leathery with the same blue eyes as Eva. They were in their sixties, fit but a little stooped. I'd seen them before in the pages of *Health and Efficiency*. They'd apparently seen us many times on the island. The thrill of meeting a couple of pensioners who enjoyed a bit of tourist-spotting was resistible. They were still smiling and laughing.

Eva let me in on the joke. 'They thought I was pregnant and that you were my husband.'

I was resplendent in my delectable high-legged trunks and a milk-coloured silk shirt split to the yoke, the tails of which were wrapped around me Yohji-style. How could anyone fail to notice I was not batting on Eva's team?

'*Ja*, we both thought Eva was pregnant *und* you were her young man.'

The trio tittered. It occurred to me that there were two quips here: either (a) Eva's bump was, funnily enough, full of poison and not a baby, or (b) Eva's supposed husband was me. I had no idea as to which of these hilarious jokes amused them so much. Surely it was the latter as I couldn't imagine Eva telling everyone on first acquaintance about her illness. They carried on with their polite and proper laughter and, between chortles, the German wrinklies invited the two of us back to their hotel. Eventually they wandered off and Eva stayed with me, silent. It got weird.

'If only it was a baby.'

'What?'

'If only it was a baby and not cancer. A baby. This big lump, it could be, couldn't it?'

Eva had clasped her stomach with both her hands and looked like a strange Madonna.

'Yeah, it's a mistake anyone could make.'

'Is it, Jake? A child? I wish it was.'

But it wasn't. Yes, wouldn't it be better if the growth were our baby? Much better – unlikely, though . . . The two of us leant against the wall outside the shop, soaking up the heat, saying nothing, feeling a little sad.

* * *

The Garden Hotel had just fallen short of the Trade Descriptions Act as its acreage had been incinerated during the long hot summer. The building was low and built of red-brick with not a Ewing in sight. It was white and spacious, cool and relaxed indoors. Karin was the receptionist, the type of woman my own mother would think of as 'thoroughly agreeable, a really nice girl'. The Gertrude-and-Gretel combo was there to meet us, as was, briefly, the Contessa. I could tell she owned the joint. She was small, skinny and tanned, and wrapped in loudly coloured silks. She sailed instead of walking and, dropping anchor for a minute, dazzled me with her gold jewellery and older history.

'What a pleasure, how nice of you to join us. Contessa di Barolo, but I think I'll let you call me Lauretta. It's so nice to be informal here, don't you think?' She made a big deal out of telling me she lived in Rome throughout the winter and hung out on Vulcano during the summer months; she'd be leaving soon, now that the season was over.

'Have you been to Roma? It's a wonderful city but too hot for me in the summer . . . You've not been? Then you must, after your trip to the islands.'

She was so grand she reminded me of myself in top bullshit mode.

'You'd love it, Jake – in fact, I insist you visit. How can you come to Italy and not see Roma?'

The difference was, she was for real: she didn't have to fool anyone. Lauretta sounded a bit like Patrick: if I'd spoken with her on the phone I'd have sworn she was a bloke.

An impressive and very drunken entrance from a Spanish bird interrupted us. She came staggering into Reception on perfect heels that were so spiky and cruel-looking they might have come out of a medicine cabinet rather than from a mere cobbler. She was gently coaxed off into another part of the hotel, as if she was a deranged family member or an overindulged retainer who needed specialist help. They obviously liked her there, but Eva and I weren't going to be given the chance to decide for ourselves. Her swearing grew fainter as they guided her out of earshot. I wondered whether she had a cell.

We were plonked on comfy overstuffed sofas near the reception desk and drinks were brought, martinis, and very good grown-up drinks they were too. For the first time in days I felt my alcohol level rise to a satisfactory degree. A line of coke would have been bliss but I could carry on dreaming.

Eva started to explain our mission to our hosts. '. . . so that is what we're doing here. Unfortunately it's not a holiday. I need to take the mud pools for the cancer, it's part of my cure, and kind Jake is helping me.'

Everyone was very genteel, nodding, *simpatico*. I felt myself getting bloody-minded, bored with the overwhelming niceness. Christ, had all this Euro-trash turned English-I'm-terribly-polite-and-middle-class-and-understanding, or was that the martini talking? I put it down to the latter and managed to sneak in another few drinks without Eva's detection before we set off for home.

Whom should we bump into? The *carabinieri*. This was getting tedious.

'You are new, what you do here?'

It was the same bravura performance, the same bloody policeman.

The difference was that this time I was feeling a little drunken. 'Don't know yet, sweetie, got any ideas?'

Eva grabbed my arm. 'Jake, I think that's enough.'

'No, I'd like to know. What do you do on your stinky little island? Perhaps our new friends could tell us.'

The two policemen stared after us as Eva and I walked on.

'I can tell you what they do, they bait faggots and scare the infirm.' I was getting too vocal.

'Jake, shut up, for God's sake. You'll get us both arrested.'

They were hurdle-bunting constabulary; their game nothing more than remedial therapy and, it has to be said, they did it rather well.

I waited until Eva had nodded off – she tended to fall asleep quite quickly – then headed to my rendezvous by the ponds with Al. I was being extra careful – I didn't want to bump into the fuzz again – so I skirted over a mound. Down below someone was sitting on a bank. I could just see a white shirt in the darkness. He was there. Fab.

MISSING YOU

The longer we stayed on the island the more offhand and seemingly aggressive the locals became – or, at least, they did with me. Was I being paranoid? I could tell they were talking about me as I sashayed down the road on my regular trips to the veg shop. There was one especially crabby old woman who always made a big theatrical show of crossing the road and herself as I approached. I wished I could speak Italian and then at least I could tell her to frig off fluently. Eva said I was imagining it, but I knew she was only saying that: she, more than anyone, was aware of what others might be thinking or saying. I missed Erin and our continuous chinwagging – I'd never missed her so much. I'd tried calling her a few times but her answerphone was always on – nothing changed.

'Hi, baby, it's me, Jake. Answer, won't you? I'm still here, I don't have a number so you can't call me back, I'll try again soon. Love you.'

I was feeling a bit homesick, even a little weepy.

'Jake, it's time for our walk. Are you ready?'

Some things with Eva were non-negotiable: bed linen, her

refusal to get in the mud, me having to bathe outside, and the timing of her walks. Each morning we'd have a mini-stroll at ten thirty then a hike in the afternoon at four when the sun was starting to wane. It wasn't unusual for us to do the whole ritual in silence, a comfortable hush that lent gravitas to the procedure. When we talked it always seemed to be idly trivial.

'You'd better pray the volcano here remains dormant, Jake.'

'Why?'

'This village is nearer to a crater than anywhere else in the world.'

'And . . .'

'And what, Jake?'

'Is that it?'

'*Ja*. The nearest.'

Eva was full of splendidly useless information.

Sometimes she looked like a visiting dignitary as we strolled towards the village; she'd look straight ahead, avoiding eye-contact with anyone we met. She was kinda regal, and I was constantly surprised that at the end of the walk she hadn't collected half a dozen posies and bouquets from grateful subjects. She might have done, had she had the requisite headgear.

MUD

A week had just about gone by, with our daily trips to the Garden Hotel, pizza in the evenings and late-night socials with the *carabinieri*. I'd got my new posse nicely lined up now: one decrepit Kraut, the Grimm twins Gretel and Gertrude, nice-girl Karin, Stefan (the flaxen beach-babe), Alessandro (by special appointment only) and the Contessa Lauretta. We were like an alternative Village People. Alcohol and fags still featured large, despite Eva's protestations. Drugs were regrettably at an all-time zero (I hadn't really expected otherwise), but the carnal department was bearing up. Apart from missing Erin, my biggest problem was money: my hundred quid was all but spent. We were gently coming to a halt, we were stagnating. I was becoming a slo-mo-sexual. Eva still hadn't got into the reeking slurry pits for her unrefined radiotherapy. The entire escapade struck me as a trip for no-go wastrels.

'Eva, don't you reckon it's time you got your butt into that medicated mud?'

'No, I don't want to.'

'I thought that was the whole reason for coming to this place.'

'It was.'

'Then let's do it, or we'll be leaving before you get round to it.'

'What? You want to do it too?'

'You're the one who wants to radiate at freakish frequencies with nature, not me. Please, just get into the bloody mud.'

Volcanic mud pools, like carrot juice, had never really appealed. They were smelly, dirty, poisonous-looking broths. What would persuade me to sit in that shit?

'Would you come with me to the pool, then, Jake?'

That would be the answer. 'If it'll get you into that cack, yes, but let's just bloody do it.'

I couldn't believe I'd agreed to it. I'm not the type of guy who's into alternative therapy, yet here I was, grudgingly agreeing to suppuration. I could see myself turning into a chunky-knit-sweater-wearing-pass-the-bean-sprouts-man-I'm-just-locating-my-ley-line hippie. I would embrace a kaftan karma and tie-dye all my clothes. God forbid, I might turn into the type of bloke who listens to Pink Floyd and thinks it groovy. I'd wear poncy beads and give peace signs to everyone I met, whether I knew them or not. So much for me being on the cutting-edge of fashion, I was yielding to the power of herbal infusions, Oriental chants and unorthodox treatments. Was I ready to take on a crash course in whale song and spiritual bongo drumming? The very idea of some choral orcal piece with a snappy rhythm section was enough to catapult me out of my right-on self-delusion. Nope, I'd just leisurely loll in the shit with Eva.

My mind switched from fantasy to reflection. Even though the entire island knew who we were, I didn't know them. It was weird to be anonymous yet recognised simultaneously. Sure, my little Vulcano gang knew me, but they didn't *know* me. Not like London and Lowlife. I was momentarily jolted. My journey was doing something else to me: it had made me question whether anyone really knew who I was.

'Jake, wake up. You're always off in your own little world, aren't you? We'll go to the ponds first thing in the morning. I think we should rise at six.'

Six a.m. may be good for some people, but not me. The only time I manage a rise at six is when I'm still wide awake from the evening before, I've got a bottle of poppers up my nose and someone else in my bed – although I didn't think Eva was mooting that type of arousal. I skulked off to my room, had a wank – we'd not discussed if masturbation was allowed in the house so I utilised the opportunity – and went to bed.

It was only half light when we got up. Everything was grey, everything looked muddy: the sky, the land, the sea and the ponds. We did a hotfoot-shuffle walk through the eerily static landscape. It was striking; there was no wind, no noise, only the most perfect stillness and hush. I'd wrapped myself up in another flighty organza creation and lent Eva a white linen duster coat for the excursion. We floated through the forlorn vista like a couple of phantoms on a cheap package deal.

When we arrived there was no one about so Eva let the duster coat drop to reveal another layer – the white chiffon scarves. She pulled those off too and stood, misshapen and bloated, in her bathing costume. Gravity, or maybe it was perspective, had played a cruel trick as her body cascaded down around her frame culminating in ankles so thick that there was no suggestion of bone beneath the flesh. It would have come as no surprise to be told that these were counterfeit legs, theatrical props sculpted from latex. I was fascinated by her limbs; they had a peculiar waxiness and translucence. She looked as grey as the ground as she eased herself slimewards and plopped into the mire. I jumped in after her and was shocked to find it so warm – in fact, it was hot. The ponds were heated by seawater that had dripped down fissures to volcanic nether-regions only to be ejaculated back into the real world as blistering mud. We got into wallowing, and, as if to spite myself, I found I enjoyed it. It was fantastic. I had to be careful, though: I didn't want to sit on a spurting fumerole for fear of scalding my own. We rubbed the steely-grey-green crap into our skin and stank like a couple of rotten eggs. It got lighter; we got smellier, muddier, lazier, happier. We were doing the one thing that any well-brought-up kid would kill for: getting dirty. It was infantile, juvenile, puerile fun. We were happy as pigs.

Then they arrived. Three strangers marched over the bank bearing towels and beach bags: two men and a woman. They must have been secret tourists as we'd not encountered them before: they were probably day-trippers.

Eva froze.

'Are you OK?'

She lay there, a bit like a swollen crocodile, her eyes just peering above the mud.

'Eva, are you OK?' I asked again.

'I don't want these people here. I don't want them to see me.'

'So what are you going to do? Have them thrown out or lie submerged in shite all day?'

She was almightily grim, part angry, part hurt that anyone should have the affront to get into the pool when she was there.

'Eva, get a life.' I thought about what I'd just said. 'The place doesn't belong to us, Eva. They're only bathing. Perhaps they've got little problems that need curing too.'

Silently Eva eyed the trespassers and I tried vainly to soothe the troubled muddy waters as we all marinated in the sulphuric soup: 'So, what are we going to do, Eva? Stay here all friggin' day? Cos I'm not.'

She made a rapid movement. It wasn't exactly gazelle-like but she got her hulk deftly out of the bog and on to the bank.

'We'd better get this mud off ourselves, Jake. Come into the sea.'

She lurched past the pools, down into the shallows and paddled; scooping up water and splashing herself, beginning to enjoy herself again.

Then she let out a small shriek, and imploded. It was a barely visible twitch that seemed to affect her whole body, a tiny shudder, an intense pain. She stumbled and I panicked. Pain wasn't supposed to be a part of the experience. What was happening? I ran to where she stood and promptly shot back out of the water, screaming myself. 'Fuck, Eva, be careful!'

The water was near boiling point and Eva's yelp was part of her acclimatisation. The sea had been heated up in the same fashion as the mud pools. Her flinch wasn't, as I had imagined, a cancer-driven squeal, but a common-or-garden scalded toe. My adrenaline rush abated.

'This is some place, Eva. First you have me suppurating in bollocking sulphurous mud and now I'm dipping myself into a boiling saline solution. Do you have any idea of what this is going to do to my skin?'

I paddled gingerly in the sea at intervals until I found water that was cool enough to get into. It was an alien experience: I'd never got into a sea that might burn me before. It wasn't a problem I associated with swimming but, then, none of the problems I was encountering related to anything I knew. I felt like I was being stripped of me, and nothing made sense any more; I was isolated, away from my life. And, right then, that feeling wasn't so bad. I moved further into the water. It was phenomenal, bath-hot sea. I sank into the ripply waves and let the stinking mud drift off my body. I felt outrageously invigorated. Eva was looking good too.

'I don't fucking believe it – look at the colour these have turned.' I felt great, but I stank and my gorgeous white Lycra trunks had turned grey. My mud-enhanced well-being was wearing off already. It was the smell more than anything else that really did me in – I was rotten.

Eva was beaming. She'd got herself a new strength from somewhere – she didn't seem to care about folk seeing her body. She'd somehow reclaimed herself, smell and all. Dipping into the mud had definitely been good for Eva's brain, but fuck knew if it was doing any good to her other regions. I was now banking on an intensive course of therapy for myself, a shampoo treatment to readjust my now unnatural pH balance and dissipate the mud-infusion stink that wafted around me. Success for my intended scouring blitz seemed unlikely, though.

'Jake, I think your little friend is back.'

He was. Alessandro had an uncommon knack of appearing suddenly.

'You been in already? I hope you've left some mud for me. It's very good for the blood, you know.'

'It's all yours, Al. What are you doing later?'

'Oh, I don't know. Maybe I see you. Maybe I don't. I don't know. I have a new special friend now. Toni.'

Eva gave me one of her arch looks.

'I'm only trying to make friends, Eva.'

'Ah, is that what you call it? I think it's a little more than friends, don't you? You have the look of a lech – a rejected lech.'

I wanted to know what he meant by having a new friend. A frigging *special* new friend. I got the impression I was being elbowed. We left Alessandro in the mud and meandered back to the villa. I went to find my hose in the back garden and scrubbed furiously at torso and trunks using an entire bottle of Flex in the process. Tragically I had been right: the smell was there to stay, my trunks were fatally knackered and my bleached hair didn't look too hot either. It had gone shit green.

'Jake, will you come indoors a moment?'

I wandered into the gloom.

'What's actually going on between you and that boy?'

I got the feeling she was jealous. She was annoyed that I'd got a distraction.

'Not that much. It's not a big deal. He's just a chum.'

She was feeling neglected or, at least, she made me feel as if I were neglecting her.

'Actually I don't know if he's even a chum any more. Nothing's going on, I promise you.'

There was silence again. I didn't feel bad – I mean, even I didn't know what was going on with Alessandro. I could see Eva turning her mind over again. She looked vaguely serene when she was digging into some private recess.

'I've decided to stay on for a while longer, Jake. I won't be going back to London just yet. I thought I'd let you know.'

MORE MONEY

Karin was at her desk in Reception when Eva and I trooped in for our regular afternoon visit at the Garden Hotel.

'Karin, do you have a telephone I could use, please?'

'*Ja*, Jake, go to the booth over there and I'll get you a line.'

I dialled my number. 'Hello, Richard, it's Jake.'

'Yes, so I can hear. Where the hell are you? You should be back by now.'

'Well, I'm not. I'm still in Vulcano and I won't be back for another week.'

'You're what?'

'I'm staying on for a while.'

Richard sounded irritated. 'What do you mean you're staying? You're only supposed to be there a week.'

'Well, it's all changed. I've got to stay on.'

'You'll bloody well get back here tomorrow or I'm firing you, Jones.'

I could feel a row brewing that was capable of turning itself into a fully fledged force-ten gale. A tornado of anger, emotion and prize-winning guilt was on the horizon.

'You've had a bloody holiday – what more could you possibly ask for?' he went on.

'Money. You're going to have to send me some more cash.'

Richard was revving up for a cataclysmic rant. I butted in: 'Do you honestly think this is a frigging holiday, Dick? You do? Well, it's not. It's a fucking disaster. I'm stuck out here with a woman riddled with cancer. Poorly, huh? And I'm trying to make the most of it. She's trying to deal with all sorts of shit and I'm not about to leave her in this fucking place just because you want me back in London. I thought she was a friend of yours, for Christ's sake. I'm staying on.'

There was a silence at the other end of the phone. Then, 'How *is* Eva?'

'Are you interested? Well, she looks a bit better than she did. I think she's a lot better, actually, but she's gotta stay a while longer. And, given the circumstances, I'm staying with her.'

The storm warning was taken down and Richard clammed up.

'I do need more money, Dick. You're going to have to wire me some *pronto*, then we'll sort this stuff out when I get back. You do understand that I can't just run off and leave her here, don't you?'

My continued absence was reluctantly accepted and the cash was pledged; it would arrive the next day. He had agreed tetchily to me staying on for another week, but in doing so he sounded more spiteful and sanctimonious than usual. I couldn't figure him out.

* * *

'Erin, answer the fucking phone. I'm in Italy, your answerphone is costing me a fortune.'

Erin picked up faster than she ever had before.

'A miracle, the lady answers.'

'Get off my case, Jake.'

'I'm really missing you, babes.'

'Oh, Jakey, me too. Sorry I missed your calls. What's happening? Are you staying on or what?'

'Yeah, I'm going to be here for another week. This whole thing is kinda crazy.'

'Well, tell me about it. What's this Eva woman like?'

'Unlike anyone I know, actually – you'd like her. I'll tell you when I get back, can't speak now, this costs so bloody much. I just wanted to say hi. Are you OK?'

'Jake, I'm fine, don't worry about me, just call me as soon as you get home.'

'I'll let you know my flight times when I've got them. It'll be soon. Love you. I'll see you later, babes.'

I was really missing her. I didn't feel right if I couldn't speak to her at least once a day. And not seeing her for a couple of weeks was starting to hurt me.

Eva and Karin were laughing together and having what looked like a duplicitous chat.

'Ah, Jake, we have just been talking about you.'

'Nice words, I hope.'

'Very funny words. Karin here has told me the rumour.'

'What rumour?'

'Everyone on the island knows about your little romance.'

'D'you mean Alessandro?'

'*Ja*, they all know and think you are a terrible man.'

'Why? Because I fucked the waiter?'

'No, not that. They can't believe you are making out with a man under the nose of your pregnant wife.'

All the strange glances and hostile looks had been put into perspective. People weren't glaring at two freaks after all: they were sympathising with a woman who had been wronged by an errant and depraved husband. All bad vibes were aimed in my direction. Word had done the rounds that I would shag anything that moved, as witnessed the other night near the ponds. The *carabinieri* could vouch for it. Eva was deemed the innocent victim of my rampant homosexuality. Me, a rampant homosexual? Yes. Her, a victim? No. Never. We pissed ourselves anyway.

The laughter attracted another guest. The Spanish girl, whose name we had discovered was Isabella, appeared, looking just a little dishevelled and obviously drunk; she was blinking as if she had just got out of bed. The amazing Isabella looked a bit like a drag queen, all swathes of black hair tumbling around a face that looked as if it had just dipped itself into a makeup bag, swished around a bit then come up for air. She'd done a good drunken lipstick that had bled into the wrinkles around her mouth – it was more Max Ernst than Max Factor. Her eye-shadow was a remarkably vibrant blue that had shot past the normal boundary and was making a spirited dash towards her hairline. Her eyes were watery and misted up with booze, so it was impossible to tell if she was laughing or crying.

She decided she wanted to laugh and lurched forward. Her vicious heels went from underneath her and she fell into an embrace with me. Her Spanish slur was inspired, not that I understood a word. She started to bat her cantilevered nylon lashes at me and rub her pneumatic knockers on my chest. This felt a bit out of place, more like it belonged to Lowlife at four a.m. over a social line of coke than in the genteel lobby of the Garden Hotel at twelve noon.

Isabella was impressively drunk; her grip got stronger and I tried to fend off her slobbery kisses. She didn't give a toss, and nor did anyone else. She draped herself over me and wanted more. She was gearing up for a superannuated snog, prior to a full coupling on the hotel carpet. I needed to escape: she was doing my reputation no good whatsoever. Think of the ignominy of it all, the embarrassment of being compromised in a revealing situation. What would people think?

'I'm a pink-blooded homosexual, for God's sake. Don't you understand? This type of thing will only lead to more rumour and spurious tittle-tattle that I might be straight.'

Isabella had got me into a half-Nelson. I wasn't moving.

'It's a nightmare, she's trying to out me as a closet heterosexual. I'm appalled. Get your hands off.'

Grappling with Isabella was like being molested by a terrier fuelled with Spanish fly; she was glued to my leg and was not going to let up. Tenacious wasn't in it. I struggled and she fought, as the episode became a spectator sport for the rest of the hotel's residents.

'Isabella, I really am gay.'

Her English was obviously as good as my Spanish.

'Karin, can you tell her to back off? I'm a poof. I have my modesty to preserve.'

'What modesty?' asked Eva.

'The little bit of modesty that wasn't pickled at my birth. Just get her off.'

The G 'n' Ts, or the Grimm twins, were now in the audience too – I have always thought that Teutonic types like a good old-fashioned sex show – and they settled down in the front row to wait for the next move. There's a contradictory erotic streak in those strictly Lutheran ladies.

'Is she like this with everyone, Karin? No wonder you try to keep her locked up. Isabella, please, fuck right off.'

Isabella released her impressive grip and I escaped, virginity intact and clothing a little rumpled.

'She only wants to be your friend, Jake.'

Where had I heard that before? I rather liked the lunatic Izzy, provided I could keep her at a safe distance.

'*Ja*, you've made a big impression on Isabella.'

'Not as big as the one she's made on me, I promise you. I've come over all queer. I think I need counselling.'

Eva and I made a getaway, lost our new chum, and headed towards the beach.

'What did Dick have to say, then?'

Suddenly it occurred to me that we hadn't really talked about Richard during the whole time we'd been away. His wobbly presence had been unconsciously exorcised from our conversation – at least, it had as far as I was concerned.

'Nothing much, he just sounded a bit weird. He gets a bit nasty, doesn't he?'

'What did he say, Jake?'

'It wasn't so much what he said as the way he said it. I had to ask him to send me some more cash and he went nuclear.'

'Well, what do you expect? You know what Dick is like when money is mentioned.' She had a point; he was miserly at best.

'But I thought he was your friend. What's his problem? He knows about your illness, doesn't he?'

Eva raised her eyebrows and waffled vaguely on about how she'd known him for years and that he'd always been a stingy shit. 'What about you, Jake?'

'What do you mean?'

'Tell me a little about you. I know you're playing around with that waiter boy, but that's not serious, is it?'

'Nope, it's not. There's nothing to say – we're not going out together. In fact, I rather think my little chum has moved on from me. He thought I was a big shot and I'd guess that he's now seen the light and realised I'm a popgun.'

Eva shrugged.

'And I've not got a full-time partner waiting for me at home. I don't seem to be very good at that type of thing.'

'What does that mean, Jake, "not really"?'

'I'm kinda seeing someone. Everything is "kinda" when it comes to me and blokes.'

'Don't you miss having someone who's there for you, Jake?'

'I do have someone. Erin. She's there for me. She's my best friend. I think I prefer friendship.'

'Is that true?'

I wanted it to be true. 'Of course. She's the only person I'll ever really be with. What about you, Eva, do you have a boyfriend?'

Unexpectedly she went silent and sucked in her already hollow cheeks. Then she said, 'No one who is that special. No, Jake, I don't have anybody waiting at home for me. Maybe that's something I miss. Or maybe you're right: perhaps it is better to have a friend rather than a lover.'

She changed the conversation. 'Erin sounds interesting, tell me about her.'

We sat down on the black sand in the shade of a fishing-boat and chatted idly. We were getting on.

'I'd like to see some of your designs, Jake. Find out how you work.'

'My designs . . . evolve. Look, if I can zap something with a glue gun and it stays stuck together it becomes an earring or a bag or a belt. At the end of the day people seem to like that crap.'

'Well, that's still interesting. Maybe we can do something together.'

'Do you design?'

'All my life.'

I knew it! Eva was one of those friends whom Richard aspired to become. She designed *real* jewellery, made with gold and precious stones. Fancy modern pieces that had interesting industrial materials factored in for good measure. I remembered him dropping her name into conversation – why hadn't I picked up on it earlier?

'Jake, it's all about reinterpreting common things and making the everyday beautiful. Don't you think so? For instance, wouldn't Teflon washers look amazing with diamond studs?'

Eva, I was beginning to understand, was a very eighties woman who'd done it all. She had gone to New York when she was twenty-four and lived loft-style long before anyone else had the idea, yawn. She stayed for ten years before she drifted into Britain and Belsize-boho-Park where she'd now been for over a decade. She had made expensive, good-taste baubles all along – hell, the V & A had some of her stuff.

'Jake, let's do something together.'

'Like what?'

'Well, let's see.'

The afternoon was spent fantasising over a conceptual joint venture. The classic design partnership Bergstrom Jones was born at about three p.m. By four o'clock I'd set up offices in Mayfair and had a staff of twelve working for me. At a quarter past I seriously considered opening a showroom in New York. At four thirty we'd designed an entire new range of virtual jewels. It brought the Milanese-faggot design supremo right back out of me. Eva bought into my make-believe.

'White ostrich is where I'm coming from, Eva. It's summery and luxurious yet very understated.'

'*Ja*, but what will you do with it?'

'I'm thinking detachable watch-straps, chokers – and as a belt it would be the season's must-have.'

'A white belt made from overgrown chicken skin will be the season's must-have?'

Eva, I realised, was cool.

'Jake, why don't we do something crazy with glue guns

and diamonds?' She was a mixture of cool and Liberace. 'Let's have some fun with this, Jakey.'

She was cool and demanding. Heck, she was undoubtedly the most demanding woman I had ever met – not that I'd met many women stuffed up with cancer before, demanding or otherwise. I liked her, even though we were so radically different. I was getting to like her company, her companionship. She was a crazy witch.

The Bergstrom Jones partnership was enthusiastic and deluded to a fault. By sundown we'd conceptualised a women's-wear range, done a diffusion line, sorted out our licencing deals and toyed with the idea of bed linens and perfumes.

'We need the pink pound, Eva, what about a poofy aftershave?'

'What will you call it?'

In bad French accent: 'Tête, Pour Homosexuel. Or plain old Head, For Fags. It's all down to the marketing, you know.'

The sun had all but gone and we were still faffing around with illusions.

'I wasn't totally straight with you earlier, Jake.'

'What do you mean?'

'You know why Dick was weird with you this morning?'

'He's tight.'

'No, there's more to it than that. He's my husband.'

Richard married to Eva? Impossible. It didn't feel right.

'You are kidding me?'

'No, it's the truth.'

I tried to imagine the two of them. 'But I thought you

said you were single, that you missed not having somebody.'

'Richard can't cope with my illness.'

His unpleasant, sniping chat with me that morning was taking on an altogether different complexion. The toe-rag had substituted me for him. He'd disowned her as a lover and reinvented her to me as a pal. What had he been thinking? Did he honestly believe that if Eva went away for a week and hung out in some stinking pool she'd get whatever it was out of her system and feel better? Did he think she would return happily to London and their joint existence because she'd had a mini-break? Bob's-your-uncle, problem solved, bye-bye cancer, welcome home, Eva. That would never work. The trip was about redemption as much as it was about getting better. It wasn't an excursion; it was to try to right Eva's wrong.

'But I don't get it, Eva.'

'I've been married to Richard for six years. He was living with me in Belsize Park until recently, but it's changed. He has always been supportive, Jake. When I first found out about the cancer he couldn't have been better. But it's all gone . . . sour.'

'He's walked out on you?'

'No, he's giving me a little space.'

'That sounds like he's walked . . .'

'Jake, it's not like that. It's hard living with cancer. It's hard for him – it's almost like it's eaten a little bit of Richard too. He's not a bad man, Jake.'

Eva looked almost tearful. Strange, really, because I knew she was the type of woman who didn't cry.

'These last three months have been particularly difficult. Everything has changed – look at me, I've changed.'

'What will happen next?'

'I don't know, Jakey. I'll wait until I get back to London.'

The sun was dying, but it was still hot and the two of us were glued to the fishing-boat.

'And what about the other friend who was going to travel with you? Was she genuine?'

'Yes, she couldn't face me either. It's a strange feeling to misplace people that you've always relied upon. It's not that they're gone for ever, they're just missing. Haven't you ever done that? Lost someone for a little while?'

No, I hadn't. I couldn't afford to lose anyone.

'I rethink my life all the time now, Jake. I find it hard to trust anyone any more.'

Nothing was as it should have been. We were sitting on the black sand and I didn't know what to say.

ISLAND LIFE

My TV career had taken off. I'd got prime-time sewn up as well as a couple of lesser gigs in the afternoon. Yep, the Jake and Eva star was now in the ascendant. We were exceptionally well received as regulars in the now well-established soap, *Garden Hotel*, and I still made my reluctant cameo appearances in *Carabinieri Vice*. I did rather well at daytime telly too: *Jake's Cakes* was a cookery show that went out every other day at lunchtime. Our mini-series existence had taken on a rhythm and schedule of its own, repeating itself along the way, and always returning to the mud pools. It was only ever the two of us who made those early-morning trips – no one else was invited: we were a couple of misfits marooned in the mire.

The scene of the action had shifted a little too. We didn't always shuffle to the Garden Hotel: instead we encouraged a reciprocal arrangement with our new friends to visit the villa, hence star billing together in our own vehicle, *Jake and Eva's Place* . . . This was more of a chat show than a drama; we were the Wogans of early-evening TV. The Grimms would come over in the late afternoon and sit on the veranda to talk in German with Eva. There was a domestic, intimate feel about their chats: it was as if the three had known each other for years, they seemed so personal. I would lie out in the sun and feel like a kid eavesdropping on his parent chatting to her friends. I felt marvellously secure. If I wasn't with them, I'd wander down to the beach and swim, sometimes bumping into Stefan and Alessandro.

'Jake, what you do today?'

'Just chilling, Al. What about you?'

'My new friend has a big yacht so today I go sailing.'

'Very nice.'

'You should see. Is got beautiful white leather and chrome. I think maybe it cost a trillion lire.'

'So I guess that leaves you and me to have a swim then, Stef.'

Alessandro headed off towards the harbour and Toni's gin palace, while Stefan and I walked over the flat black sand into the deep, still sea.

Occasionally the afternoon conversation between the Germanic triumvirate was in English and Eva would gas about a friend of hers called Maria, who lived on an island nearby.

'I think it would be nice to visit Maria, Jake. Do you fancy that?'

'Perhaps we could stay a day or so on the way home.'

'I'd better track her down, then, let her know we'd like to come.'

I wasn't quite sure how she was going to 'track her down', but for all the crap that had been thrown at this woman, her confidence was supreme. It was as if she'd got a cosmic hotline: she could do anything, as long as it was slowly. Slowness was a part of life now. The island had its own time, it was all a little stretched out, languorous and unto itself. An hour often lasted an entire afternoon, just like the way time had stretched when I was a child: then the idea of tomorrow might as well have been next year. It was like that on Vulcano. I felt like I'd been on the black sands for months.

Isabella started to hang out at the villa too. Poor, fabulous, demented Izzy got progressively more drunk and outlandish-looking every day. She might have been the subject of a natural-history programme: she was animalistic, reliant upon her pre-programmed drunken wits. Each year her rich industrialist husband dropped her off on Vulcano, abandoning her on the black sands, while he sailed around the Mediterranean presumably enjoying himself on his yacht while she got more and more deranged in her luxury prison. The island had that effect – I think we all felt a little mad, forgotten, quarantined on Vulcano.

Isabella was the loneliest person I'd ever met. I could see it in her face. Beneath the Barbara Cartland School of Makeup Application was beauty. It was barely detectable under her slick of blue eye-shadow; but it was in her eyes. She was like a mirror and I was looking at a bit of me. But now she had found new friends in us – not that we could communicate effectively. She focused on joining in, adopting her I'm-slightly-pissed-but-not-really-that-much-and-I'd-love-to-be-a-nurse role. Who were we to refuse her this small pleasure? She was harmless, invariably funny and as hungry for companionship as both Eva and I. We all knew that instinctively.

* * *

My extra week had elapsed, but neither Eva nor I referred to it. We had our circle, we had our mud baths, Eva had her carrot juice, and we got on with living. Lunches were at home, suppers were sometimes out, as often as not at the pizzeria. Stefan was always there. He was a good-looking man; I listed him in my *filo* section. Strange, really: it was unlike me to put a guy like that straight into the safe bit. I liked him, but that was it, it felt kinda good. One evening, after a dozy meal with Eva, Stefan escorted us, rather than the *carabinieri*, on our shuffle home through the aloe and the rocks. We dropped Eva off at the villa and decided to go for a midnight swim. Everything was black, water, beach and sky, except for the most stupendous explosion of stars. We splashed into the warm sea, and as we swam we could see starry reflections in the water around us, trails of them, blooms of them.

'It's like I'm stoned, Stef.'

'What?'

'Just look in the water. It doesn't look real.'

I wasn't stoned, it was real – and it wasn't reflections. We were caught up in phosphorescence. It was magical. Two slightly drunken guys effervescing in water and the most fabulous light show on earth. It was damn near perfect.

After bed-making origami hell, the night-time was invariably plagued by insects from Hades. The villa, and especially my room, became Mosquito Central. I would lie awake in the dark listening for Eva's swearing and slaps in the next room and the piercing sound of the microlight aircraft used by the mozzies in mine. It was a futile battle; we were never going to repel the marauders. It was getting to be too much; next morning I was on ***repellent awareness***.

'That's fine for you, Jake, but I'm not having that stuff anywhere near my body. Keep it away from me, and you won't spray it around here either.'

'That's cool, Eva. You suffer, then.'

I minced off to what I thought was the right place. The regimented shelves and stock were so sparklingly clean and bright, I couldn't help but think pharmacy. I was wrong; it was a supermarket that looked medicated. It didn't stop me from doing a camp little mime routine to get directions to the chemist. There, I started my mosquito impression once again to the bemused assistants and produced a startlingly real sound effect, rounding off with a little self-flagellation at the end. I was given a lurid yellow bottle with a picture not only of a dead mozzie on the front but the entire entomology of the island, including a variety of scarab-like beetles and a gruesome-looking millipede. The detailed instructions, in Italian, were punctuated with skull and crossbones. It was just what I wanted. It looked as if it was going to be noxious and chemical enough for my purposes. I was happy.

But on my return Eva was not. 'I've told you, that stuff is disgusting. Keep that poison away from me.'

'You're not going to be using it. Relax. It's different for you anyway.'

'Why is that?'

'Because you'll reap a bitter revenge on the little fuckers.'

'What do you mean?'

'It's quite simple. When they've done their utmost in biting you they're going to fly off into the night and drop dead the next morning of mozzie cancer.'

Eva laughed. That night, after a boozy-ish supper, I put the synthetic elixir to the test. I splashed the stuff all over me as if I were applying Tête, Pour Homosexuel in a crappy atmospheric aftershave commercial. I dumped the bottle on the bedside table and heard it fall over as I switched out the light. I couldn't be arsed to pick it up.

The tiny buzz of the first raider. Silence. There was another irritating whine, then the silence of it cutting out mid-flight. Moz-O-Gone was the dog's bollocks: it just killed the little blighters outright before they even had the chance to get to me. I was thrilled. The mosquito murderer fell into a deep and contented sleep. Next morning I awoke without any bites (hooray), no hangover (hoo-fucking-ray) and no alarm clock. I did a double-take. The clock was now just a pool of black plastic muck on the bedside table; the bottle of Moz-O-Gone had leaked in the night and melted it. What was the lotion going to do to me? I decided the incident was probably best kept from Eva. I had a hunch that she might not understand my point of view.

LOBSTER

Eva had gone on a bit of a mission: she was trying to contact her old chum Maria without a phone number or an address. Because of the nature of the islands it took her little time to locate a local who knew exactly where Maria lived and, not only that, he'd take a message to her the following day. Eva was thrilled with her detective work; I was less thrilled with Eva. She was looking grey: an indefinable frailty had crept in – unnoticed till now.

'Are you OK, Eva?'

'Mmm?'

'Is everything OK with you?'

'*Ja*. Why do you ask? Do I look like I'm going to drop dead on you? What's worrying you?'

'Nothing, I was just asking, that's all.'

I was anxious. She didn't look well.

Eva stared at me with a small smile. 'Jake, you silly boy, I'm not going to die just yet, believe me.'

I felt like hugging her; I just wanted to hold on.

'You're very sweet, Jake, for all your craziness. Thank you.'

I felt like she was letting me in. There was no more

hostility or witchiness from her or me. We had unexpectedly become friends . . . good friends. It was like the time in the amusement arcade on that shitty Sunday afternoon when I met Erin. Imperceptibly something had snapped, and we had clicked. Right then, that very instant, I felt like I was a best mate.

Isabella, bless her, wanted to take Eva and me out for dinner. It was her special treat, but it also felt like she was sneakily rehabilitating herself (I was under the distinct impression she was verging on sober). Vulcano wasn't overly blessed with restaurants, especially since the season was over. Apart from the pizzeria and the Garden Hotel there wasn't much else other than the Casa Becci – which was closed – and a shack just off one of the beaches. It was here that Izzy wanted to take us.

I couldn't say I was excited at the prospect of dinner with her, as, at best, conversation was bound to be surreal. Izzy would have to translate her Spanish badly into German, which could then be relayed to me in English. I imagined I would try to flirt with the waiter in hopeless Italian. The United Nations we were not.

At dusk Izzy came over to the villa and we hobbled to the restaurant on the beach. It really was a shack: we walked straight through it into a sandy, desiccated garden at the back. A skinny tree stood in the middle of the dining area and a few potted plants were strewn around the tables. We sat down at a table in the middle, underneath what we could now see was less an anorexic tree than a neurotic shrub – it had started to go bald and most of its leaves were under our table. A wire ran from the hut to a branch and a bare lightbulb dangled below it. About half a dozen others were dining there that night too, and they all stopped to look at us when we, a trivet of freaks, tripped in. I guess we were now inured to the rustic fascination shown by everyone on Vulcano. It didn't even raise a blip on Eva's radar.

Izzy wanted to spoil us and ordered what she said would be a spectacular lobster. That was the lie of the place: the venue looked impoverished and the best I'd thought we could hope for was an authentic spag bog, but the menu offered lavish seafood and truly fab wines – with prices to match, natch. It must have been one of the first trendy peasant eateries in the universe, wellington-boot chic before its time. I was getting into it all. The restaurant scene felt like a thing of the past, so the excitement of being in one now – other than Pizza Paradise – was geeing me up. Izzy ordered the wine, which arrived quickly.

I lit up a fag, slugged down a delish glass and earned a disapproving look from Eva. 'Jake, do you have to?'

'What?'

'You must stop smoking, I can't bear it.'

'I will, I promise, when we get back to London,' I lied.

Izzy was getting flirty with me. I had visions of her tampering with me again and demanding a good servicing as a post-dinner amusement. I was thankful I was wearing trainers – at least I could make a quick getaway.

The vibe was great, Izzy was funny even in translation, the evening flowed. The first bottle of wine vanished quickly and a second was ordered; we were enjoying ourselves. The guy who'd taken our order eventually arrived with the biggest, most Baroque lobster I'd ever seen. It was the type of beast that prompted an 'ooh' or an 'aaah' from everyone in the restaurant: it was a yard long, all curly antennae and orangy-red armour plating. I wanted to clap. It was much better than a birthday cake could ever be.

As it was put on the table Eva groaned and slumped to one side, then slid to the floor. Hell and a half broke loose. I leapt to my feet and knelt beside her, the lobster went flying, Izzy howled, the waiter ran, the other diners were staring. Eva just groaned. ***Eva awareness***: she was dying, I knew it. She was going to die. A mixture of thoughts ran through me simultaneously: I've-gotta-getta-cab-she's-fucking-dying -wish-Isabella-would-shut-up-she-can't-bloody-die-better-light-a-fag-get-a-cab. I felt thrilled. It was a mixture of terror overridden by pragmatism. ***Reality check twelve***: I had to solve the situation; I had to save Eva.

I ran out of the building and fled towards the harbour. I needed a taxi. The port was quiet, the whole frigging island was quiet, the automobile was still a dream of the future. One of the knackered harbour buildings was full of local men. It was, I guess, a kind of caff-cum-bar, a sort of working-men's club. I ran inside, panting; the rest of me fluttered and billowed in behind. Right then a poncy shirt wasn't a good thing. I had just made a very big entrance. I shouted for a taxi. '*Pronto, amigo malade, pronto, pronto.*'

I was living proof of it: the poof they'd all seen wandering around the island was insane. Not only was he a cross-dressing undesirable and the pervert father of Eva's unborn child, he was illiterate in Italian to boot. I shouted more; I pleaded for a taxi. Eventually a bloke got up to help.

'Taxi *perfavore, pronto, restauranti pesce, pronto, pronto.*'

It was patently obvious that something other than me was up and Cabman ushered me to his car. I steered him towards the shack and ran inside. Eva was still slumped on the floor, Isabella was still howling, the waiter didn't know what to do and the other diners were in a state of intense, yet detached fascination. Cabman and I managed to get Eva up, walk her gently to the car and ease her on to the back seat. Everything felt profoundly still. We drove slowly back to the villa, leaving Isabella at the shack gulping what remained of the wine. The excitement had put paid to her abstinence. Not that I cared: I was ready for a syringeful of smack. Chase the dragon? Fuck, I'd scarper after a lizard provided it altered the situation. Everything would be fine, I lied to myself.

Cabman didn't want paying. He was kind. Maybe he thought her waters had broken and the happy couple, their celebratory supper curtailed, would be planning a helicopter airlift to Palermo for a joyous delivery. Maybe he thought we were going to do it ourselves with Marigolds, a couple of sheets, a bottle of *grappa* and a nice hot kettle for that well-deserved post-natal cuppa.

I got Eva on to the origami bed where she lay and moaned. I couldn't figure out which was louder: Eva groaning or the silence. I sat a little way from her in the darkness and tried to speak. It was useless: she was enveloped in pain. Everything was black, sticky and paralysed. Time was stretching again. For hour after hour the incessant silence was lifted only by deathly moans and overwhelming pain. It was like sitting with Munch's *The Scream*, except this one was louder. I sat and sat, all through the night. I was powerless. I hated it. Eventually the gloom in the villa was marginally lifted by grey sunlight from outside. It felt as though this shadowy existence might last for ever. It was as if the day would never break – we were to be left in a no man's land. We were frozen into a part of history that wasn't anything. The world was impotent, helpless, awful and dying. By eight that morning I'd had it.

'Eva . . . Eva, I'm just going out for a swim. Can you hear me? I'm just going for a swim. I won't be long, just a few minutes.'

Her hulk remained static: she wheezed. I walked down to the beach. There was no sun, just a blanket of cloud. The sky was grey, the beach and sea black: the island had turned into gun-metal. The stillness I had noticed at the shack the previous night was still apparent, furious now in its intensity: I could almost feel it on my face. I walked into the sea, surprised again by how warm the cold, dead-looking waters were, and started to swim slowly, curious because the water was flat – not even a ripple. It started to drizzle. I was stuffed up with emotion, desperate, horrified that Eva wasn't getting better. As I swam, the weirdest thing happened: as if on cue someone in a far-off villa cranked up Vivaldi's *Four Seasons*, the pretty music bouncing off the still waters then racing past me. I was crying. Fucking great big sobs. They were Louis tears that had come back unexpectedly – I was choked. I was struggling to work out what to do, how to banish her pain.

I found it.

There was only one thing I could do: I had to kill her. She was dying. Hell, this was some realisation. She was going to die on me. This was the moment I had been assured wouldn't happen. There was no going back now and just one thing for me to do. The only way I could help her was to finish her off, snuff her out. I had to put her down.

I swam back to shore, tried to pull myself together, then headed for the Garden Hotel. Karin was there. 'Can I use the phone, please?'

'*Ja*, I'll get you a line.'

I called Erin. 'Baby. It's me. Answer the phone. Answer the fucking phone, will you? Please, babes.'

All I got were the pips from the answerphone.

I tried Richard. 'You gotta help me, Dick.'

'What's going on, Jones, and where the hell are you?'

'I'm going to kill Eva. You're going to have to help me.'

'*What?*'

'I'm going to kill your wife.'

There was a chasm of silence.

'I'm going to kill her. She's dying. There's nothing else for it. I'm going to kill her, you asshole.'

I could see Karin looking at me interestedly. She could see my hysteria but the glass booth muffled the sound effects. It must have been like watching a passionate episode of *Dynasty* with the mute button on.

'What are you bleating about, Jake? Are you pissed?'

I detonated, emotional and crazed, and demanded he got the next flight out to Sicily because I was going to end up in prison courtesy of the psychotic *carabinieri* – all because the job of butchering his dying spouse had been left to me. It was more terrible than I could imagine: someone I loved was fading from me, and the business of her falling over the edge wasn't going to be natural.

I had to push her. 'Just get your fucking arse out here, Dick.'

'Out where?'

'Call the Garden fucking Hotel for details. I'm sure they'll know which prison I'll be in.'

I hung up and made a dash for it from the booth. Karin shouted after me, realising that the purple episode of hammy acting she'd just seen might just have been the real thing. I ran out of the hotel, still crying, wearing my knackered trunks and a now very grubby-looking Tom of Finland T-shirt, not the get-up one would expect of an assassin. I was headed back to the villa.

As I neared, I slowed down. How *was* I going to kill her? How do you kill anyone? Where do you start? I'd never thought about murder before. If I'd got a gun then I could have sneaked in, pulled the trigger and watched my victim's brain hurl itself against the wall. It would be easy, wouldn't it? I didn't think so. What the fuck? I didn't have a gun. I could strangle her. Maybe that wouldn't be so bad. I'd have to dig my fingers deep into her throat and squeeze. But there would be a terrible struggle. We'd end up having a fight, and I couldn't cope with that. There was no rolling-pin for me to thwack her with. I needed a knife. The only weapon with any clout in that poky-frigging place was a knife.

I walked quietly into the kitchen and slid open the drawer. Where the fuck were the knives?

There, beside the tea strainer, the wooden spoons and the garlic-crusher, was my weapon, a bread-knife that was not exactly glinting in the morning gloom. It was serrated, rusty and the blade bent slightly when it was cutting. It would have to do. In my madness I felt like a Dynastic Joan Collins. I was a diva in a melodrama. I could see Alexis now, scrabbling through a kitchen drawer, a little bit pissed, trying to find her weapon – a decorative letter-opener; she'd hide it in the fold of a sable coat. Blake Carrington would be working at his desk, his back towards her. Her stilettos are silent on the marble floor, the knife, on show now, slowly rising above her head. I could see Joan's weapon: it wasn't a letter-opener, it was a shiny silver dagger. I felt sick.

I held the bread-knife behind my back and crept slowly into the living room; there in the middle was Eva's abstract hulk under her grey blanket. She looked very still, not at all like Blake doing his accounts. Where did I start? What the fuck would Joan do? The idea of stabbing Eva was too appalling to contemplate, the image of her pressurised belly exploding and propelling a mass of cancerous guts across the floor too frightful. Should I try to stab her in the back or plunge the blade into her chest? It wasn't going to work. Joan had a dagger and all I had was a Bendy Toy knife that would have difficulty in puncturing a slice of Mother's Pride, let alone a ribcage. I decided to start sawing at her neck. It would be quick, wouldn't it? How long does it take to decapitate a person with a bread-knife? I sidled up behind Eva, heart beating, almost blind with fear.

She swung over and glared at me. 'Where have you been?'

'What?'

'I said, where have you been? How long does it take for a swim now?'

I was mumbling: 'I've been to the hotel.' I was panicking.

'Well, I'm glad you're back. What have you got behind you?'

'Nothing.'

The killing thing wasn't panning out: I'd imagined her in a semi-coma by now, prostrate, incoherent and ready for the fatal blow, not quizzing me as to where I'd been for the past hour or so.

'No, go on, what have you got?'

'Nothing.' I could feel tears welling.

'No. What is it? Stop hiding from me, Jake.'

'It's a knife.'

'What?'

'It's a fucking knife – to kill you.'

'To what?'

'I've come to kill you. I can't stand to see you like this, what else can I do for you?'

Eva was laughing; my tears were splatting on to the floor.

'I didn't know what else to do – you're dying.'

'Me? Dying? I don't think so.'

My sobs and her laughter were getting louder.

'It was wind, terrible wind, Jake. When you'd gone off to swim I farted like never before. And that was it. The pain vanished.'

I looked dumb. Eva was still laughing. Her pain had gone. She'd done a botty-burp and blown last night's agony and this morning's cause for murder out of her body. She laughed and I cried.

I felt hysterical. 'But I've told Dick what I'm going to do.'

'You've done what?'

Eva was about to kill herself laughing.

'I told him I was going to kill you.'

'So do you have to do it now, Jake? Please, stop making me laugh, I can't bear it.'

My tears were still flowing, but they'd swapped from tragedy to comedy.

'Are you going to call him back and tell him I've farted?'

'I suppose I should.'

I felt foolish and decided it would probably be better if I called a bit later. I'd got Karin to contend with as well.

CARLOS THE JACKAL

The entire island had heard about the shack incident. Various interpretations were doing the rounds, including eyewitness reportage from Izzy, the layman's point of view from Cabman and a tabloid take on events from Karin. She'd observed the scene in the phone booth without understanding the content of my conversation, but had had the bonus of Richard calling back in a frantic panic, muttering about *carabinieri* and stopping Jake's mercy mission. Nobody knew about the rusty bread-knife and murderous intent; as far as everyone was concerned, Eva's ordeal had been her collapse. It altered everything, though: our forays to the Garden Hotel became less frequent because suddenly its inhabitants were making more regular and recurrent visits to our villa. We had become quite the *cause célèbre*. The entire day after the event was littered with people dropping by to get the gen – even the Contessa came. The islanders regarded the patient – who, in both her and my eyes, had now recovered – as even more infirm and fit for sympathy. It didn't matter how many times we told the G 'n' Ts, Karin and Izzy that she'd farted and it was all OK now, they still saw a sick woman. I didn't. I saw a bloody-minded woman. I saw a living, go-for-it woman. I saw her beauty.

'Jake, I'm ready to get off this island. What do you think?'

'Where are we going? Back to London?'

'Why don't we go to Maria for a few days? Then we'll think about going back to London.'

'Whatever happens I'll have to get back soon. Fuck it, yeah, let's go and visit Maria.'

It didn't take much to persuade myself as to the advantage of not returning straight away. Eva's previous detective work had produced an address for Maria, and the go-between had warned her of our intention. It was up to us to get our arses over to Stromboli. We mentioned the idea to Karin, who felt that we should stay put. The grannies and the Contessa freaked when they heard that we were off.

'My dear, look at how difficult that journey will be. You must stay with us for a while yet.'

'That's very kind of you, Contessa, but Eva and I have decided that we are leaving.'

'You can't possibly. She's so ill. I'd never be able to forgive myself if anything should happen.'

The Contessa wasn't naturally selfish, although that's how she sounded. She had simply reached a state into which we all inevitably fall when dealing with another's misfortune. It has nothing to do with the sufferer and everything to do with guilt. But nothing the Contessa, or anyone else for that matter, could say would alter our objective. Why should it? Somehow Eva and I had become self-contained. Through our walks, mud baths and time together I'd found something deeper:

we were together, we were fine, there weren't going to be any problems that we couldn't deal with. Fuck it, we were two happy freaks who wanted out of there.

The Garden Hotel decided to throw a dinner in our honour. There was something vaguely incongruous about it: it felt like the Last Supper, which it most definitely was not. A long table was set out in the foyer, with Eva and myself at opposite ends and the grannies, Karin, Izzy, the Contessa and her three adult children – they'd popped over for the weekend – in the middle. It was a faintly glamorous event, as if it were from another time: the type of party that, had it been photographed, would be sepia and a little crumpled. It was also charged with emotion: our new pals were upset at our departure. It felt as if we were leaving Heathrow all over again, with Eva's friends fussing around. It had an air of finality. But this time I was involved: I was part of the ritual. Eva and I needed to escape from all this. We left with a chorus of goodbyes and *arrivederci*s and please-come-back-and-visit-us-here's-my-address-in-Germany-write-to-me-soons. I kicked myself: I'd forgotten to bring my Filofax.

We headed along the dirt track, past the cacti and straight into the police.

'Papers, please.'

'I beg your pardon?'

'You give me your papers.'

This was a new one on us.

'Which paper is it you want? Eva, I believe you still have a copy of the *Guardian* and, if I'm not mistaken,

I'm pretty certain I've got a selection of *Smash Hits* from 1981.'

Our constable friends were as long of face as they were of arm.

'You report tomorrow with your papers.'

'Can't wait, darlings. It's a date. I'll shoosh myself up for it.'

Eva was silent.

The swine let us go, as they always did, and we walked on. Eva was getting a bit vinegary. By the time we'd got back to the villa she was positively acid. We packed up as many of our belongings as possible, then went to our respective beds. By now she was in a very shitty mood.

It was an early start and I wandered along to the harbour to track down Cabman. This time I wasn't wearing a Tom of Finland erection or one of my blousy silk numbers. I'd decided to go out in civilian wear or, at least, as plain-clothes as the cut-off rent-boy jeans would ever be. When I found him we headed back to base to pick up Eva, the luggage and the juice machine. Everything I did was wrong; she was getting on my tits. What was this? Jealousy? Was she pissed off because I was floating around the island without cancer? I could outdo her in clothes, but I could never know what her cancer felt like. How could I? I couldn't figure her out: she was reverting back to the prickly woman I'd met at terminal three. She was giving up on me.

We got the Aliscafi and made the short hop to Lipari. When I'd picked up our tickets in Vulcano I was warned that we'd have to make a bit of a dash to our connecting boat, which would be on the opposite side of the harbour. And not only was it a bit of a drag: the vessel would be leaving at pretty much the same time as we arrived. I warned Eva of this and got a monosyllabic reply.

'You're going to have to shuffle a bit quicker. I've got all the frigging luggage and I can't carry you as well.'

She wasn't responding.

'Eva, I don't know what's bugging you, but you're going to have to help me out here.'

We got off the boat and started to make our way around the quayside, the cases and Eva's sodding juicer clanging around me. Eva skulked behind. We had turned into a parodic couple, the couple that sulked, albeit the couple that didn't know why. We headed towards the next vessel.

'*Scusi.*'

I looked round: Lipari's *carabinieri* had decided to acquaint themselves with me. How kind. What an expected non-pleasure. The surprise quotient was zero. ***Reality check thirteen***: they were going to be fuckers. More than fuckers. They wanted to search me in their shitty caravan tucked on the far side of the harbour. Time was strictly limited. If I missed the boat we could always get another – in three days' time. I started to put up a fight.

'My boat is about to leave, whaddya want with me?'

'Step this way.'

'Don't you understand? My boat is trying to leave and I've got to get on it.'

I was bundled into the shed with wheels. They didn't give a monkey's – and, by the look of her, neither did Eva. It was all guns and bravura, much like my original mental impression of the trip except that I wasn't smuggling cocaine for Richard, I was doing a nice line in cancerous contraband instead. The first cop behaved like he'd caught Carlos the Jackal; he was way too *Starsky-and-Hutch*-legs-apart-piece-out-and-ready to look even remotely cool. I looked on in disbelief. I was verging on laughter at the antics of the parochial peacekeepers, before being consumed by rage. I was really pissed off.

'Will you let me fucking go?'

It wasn't going to happen. They knew exactly what they were doing even though they didn't understand me and I didn't understand them. Robo-cop was getting more bullish and had decided to go through my possessions. He ignored Eva's luggage and the precious juicer that, with a little imagination, might easily have been an atomic trigger – perhaps not – and opened my battered case. He flicked open the locks and looked visibly startled by the array of chiffon and organdie he'd flushed out; it was hardly daywear for an international terrorist. I guess he'd formed other ideas. I was Carlos the Dragal. I had been singled out as a cross-dressing drug smuggler. Draglos the Drugal. Tucked into a small inside pocket of the case was a conker. First Pig had found it and held it aloft in triumph.

'Hashish?'

'No, conker.'

'Hashish . . .'

'No, fucking conker.'

It got ugly. First Pig got out a knife and started to cut the stitching on my bag. He was slashing the leather of my beautiful old case and pulling out the kapok stuffing. I was getting really fucking mad.

'Leave it alone.'

He was a bully and he was enjoying it. I felt like sobbing; but I was fucked if I was going to blub in front of a prize shit.

'Hashish.'

'Are you really that frigging stupid? Since when has a conker even remotely resembled a lump of dope? Go and smoke it and see what good it does you.'

The bastard carried on decimating my precious case.

'It's a conker, for Christ's sake.'

Eva had now appeared in the caravan doorway, casting a shadow over the confusion. I wasn't sure if she'd come to gloat or rescue me. She looked ominous and suddenly seemed much bigger than the sum total of a lump and her skinny skeletal frame.

'What are you doing? The boat is about to leave – get out here now.'

Eva, in her own world, had no concept of my plight, or if she did she wasn't letting it affect her reality. She looked at me as if I was horsing around with a couple of mates, teenage and delinquent. She looked exasperated. Even more innards were pulled from my case: it was being ripped apart.

'Will you leave it alone? There's nothing there.'

'Hashish.'

'How many fucking times? It's a bloody conker.'

'Jake, we have to go – don't they know I'm ill?'

'Hashish.'

'Conker.'

'Cancer – *cancro*.'

The *carabinieri* looked puzzled. Drugs-and-drag was one thing, but a weird-looking woman shouting 'Crab,' was something else. We all had our own agenda. It was getting frantic. A French guy showed up at the caravan door looking for directions.

'Do you speak English?'

'*Oui*.'

'And Italian?'

'*Si*.'

'Thank You, God. You've got to help me.'

I pulled the fella into the caravan to join us in our lunacy. There were now four cops, a transvestite terrorist, a demented crab woman and a pesky little Frenchman all prised into the tiny space. It was hot and impulsive. I was feeling quite high. I pleaded with my new ally to tell the *carabinieri* that their drugs bust was nothing more than a conker. Cancer. Crabs. Confusion. I explained to him that I'd been in Paris and had walked along the Champs-Élysées by the horse-chestnut trees, and had picked up one of their innocent fruits and kept it. It was a souvenir that I'd put into my now totally knackered case and which I'd forgotten about. 'You do understand me, don't you? It's a nut. It's not hashish – I mean, how fucking amateur can you get?'

We were all fevered, but Eva was demented: the boat was about to leave, the cops were still fingering what was left of my case and the French bloke was still translating English into Italian. There was a gradual look of defeat on the *carabinieri*'s faces; not even they could keep me any longer. It was a nut-roast, not a drugs bust; the excitement was over.

I rushed thanks to my French saviour as I gathered up the remains of my case and my crumpled clothing. I scowled at my interrogators, grabbed Eva and shot off as fast as a shuffle would take us to the boat. My adrenaline was pumping at an all-time high. We boarded, and the vessel slipped port. Eva was incandescent; I felt void. I think she thought I'd pulled that stunt on purpose; that I'd suddenly made it my mission to thwart her journey, been in on some sort of weird joke with the cops and had needed to make a big guest appearance in the limelight. She was feeling sorry for herself, but I was feeling sorrier for me. I left her to stew in the air-conditioned bowels of the boat and went back to do serious work on my tan on the top deck. I sat and watched as Lipari and the pigs from hell got smaller and smaller. It was very sunny; I could have done with a drink but I couldn't be bothered to look for a bar and, anyway, I didn't want to bump into Eva.

We'd visited another island and let a few more passengers on and off by the time Eva came to find me. She arrived just as we swept up alongside the back of Stromboli, all dry lava and ash, monumental and awesome. This place looked more dangerous than Vulcano: there were fresh lava flows that had seeped into the ocean, huge, sterile, terrible swathes of new rock. It looked like nature hated itself.

'Jake? Are you OK up here?'

'I'm fine.'

'I'm sorry for earlier. You know that?'

Sure I did. I felt I was beginning to understand a whole lot more about everything and especially about my tricksy relationship with Eva. She wanted to tell me about the island. She was secretly excited to be there and her suppressed enthusiasm made her look almost girlish. She'd also come to make peace. We'd both calmed down now, the awfulness of the morning had vanished and everything was cool again.

The boat docked near a steep concrete slipway but was too large to get close. An islander came out in a small rubber dinghy to pick us up. He seemed to find his way instinctively and didn't look at any of his passengers. It was like he was blind. I looked at him, though: his lips had sunk into his face, forming a soft pink crater. Eva and I, a couple of other people, the luggage and the juicer were transferred to the inflatable. It was not a stable craft: it lurched wildly as each of us boarded; not that the sea was choppy. The boatman steered us to shore, where Eva and I plonked ourselves down on a bench as he and the two other passengers shot off into nowhere.

The big boat churned away from us.

'What next, Eva?'

'Let me get my breath back.'

Stromboli struck me as even more primitive than Vulcano. This was Hicksville-super-strength, urban-lite, rustic-plus. There were no taxis – in fact, no cars were to be seen. There were tractors, though. At least, there were tractor tracks. We dozed in the sun, until the rattle of antediluvian farm machinery broke the peace. I hailed it and stuck Eva, our possessions and myself on the trailer at the back.

We jerked our way along a dirt track, surrounded by scrappy sacks, a dog, a bale of hay, an enormous coil of rope and the baggage. We were spotted by a few locals and clearly amused them. I waved, then Eva waved, and we started to laugh.

Our noble transport rattled its way through meandering tracks and ancient lanes until we arrived at a smallish white-washed house. It was Maria's place, and our friendly farmer delivered us to the door. We knocked, and Maria answered. She looked as if she'd seen a ghost.

MARIA

'Eva? Is that you? Oh, my dear girl . . .'

The reunion between Eva and Maria was loving, tearful and terrible all at the same time. They hugged and clung and squeezed each other, pulling themselves into the house.

'After all this time, Eva. I'm so happy you're back on Stromboli. I never thought you'd come home.'

'Don't be silly – how could I stay away for ever?'

Eva and Maria hadn't seen each other for a third of a lifetime. Their friendship had been put into cold storage for two decades, hidden at the back of their minds. But they couldn't have been happier to find each other again. Fuck, I felt a thrill at their refound intimacy. Their friendship was invincible. They were plunged immediately into deep conversation, and it was as if the gap since their last meeting had been three months rather than twenty years, or however many it was.

'Maria, your hair, it's gone quite white.'

'I'm seventy-one years old – what do you expect?'

Eva looked almost resentful that her friend had got older – maybe she was angry about her own mortality.

'Now, Eva, don't be so silly – we all get older.'

There was still a disbelieving look on Eva's face: she couldn't quite take in that Maria was an old woman.

We were led into the house. Maria lived in Spartan luxury – she had an upper-middle-class take on rusticity. Her home was furnished with yokel simplicity that had cost a lot of money. (Only the rich can afford impeccable peasant taste.) The house was uncomplicated and surprisingly dark, even though the walls were whitewashed, as were the floors. The building seemed to go on for ever, deep into the side of the volcano. The water was pulled up from a well that had a room all to itself. I looked over the edge into a fathomless, pitch-black, echoing shaft that plunged, like the house, into the mountainside. The building was cool. We sat down at a crude table in another dark room; there was a blaze of light from outside shining through a slit in a closed shutter. I knew where I wanted to be and it wasn't inside.

'Eva, is everything OK? You don't look so well.'

The story of Eva's illness was told again. But the response wasn't what either Eva or I anticipated.

'You're a very sick woman, you can't stay here.'

'Maria, I've come to see you, what do you mean I can't stay?'

'You need specialist treatment, I can't do anything for you here. You must go to the mainland for help. Straight away.'

It was as if Eva's disease had only just been diagnosed and Maria was the first peson to be let in on the terrible secret.

'You've got to go for treatment today. You can't stay here.'

'I'm not going anywhere. I'm looking after myself very well.'

Maria seemed dazed by the revelation, dizzy with information that she hadn't wanted to hear and hatching emergency plans in a bid to resolve her long-lost friend's dilemma.

'Maybe we can get you on a boat today. Jake, you run to the harbour and ask about charters.'

'Maria, you're not listening. I don't need hospitals or treatment. I'm fine.'

'We must get you to the doctor.'

'I'm not going anywhere, Maria. Will you please listen to me?'

Maria looked frightened, impotent, and was panicking. She was feeling what I had felt during the long night that Eva lay and moaned, the night when I thought she would die. But Maria had no shared history with the sick Eva: she'd only known her as a healthy young woman. She continued to try to persuade Eva to leave the island. She was trying to be strong and motherly, but she looked weak, exhausted, and was unable to concentrate on the misfortune she had just learnt about.

'Maria, aren't you going to show us to our rooms?'

For a second she looked blank and brushed at her apron, smoothing it around her plump body. It was as if she was trying to clean away Eva's cancer like so many crumbs. Then she said, 'Oh, yes. You stay in your old room. Come on.'

She led us across a small, dazzling courtyard to another building, up some stone steps and into a beautiful light-filled room. It was a *House & Garden* space: it had big windows and rural purity in its stone walls and wooden furniture. All the colour had been eaten away by the sun. There were two beds, a small wash-basin, a couple of cupboards and a stone bathtub with shower. It was fab. I went to find the luggage that had been dumped in the hall.

I walked back into the room with the bags and the sacred juicer. Eva and Maria were hard at it again, catching up on two decades of news.

'Have I changed that much, Eva? I don't feel any different.'

'We've both changed.'

'The only difference is age. I don't look in the mirror any more. I don't recognise the old lady who looks back at me. But that's the only difference, white hair and lines. My heart is still the same. I'm still the same Maria who brushed your hair, who kissed your cheek.'

'You're right. I only have to look into the faces of others to see the change in me. But it is only the outside. Maria, I'm so glad to be back here.'

It struck me that trying to hurry through twenty years of change was the same as myself meeting up with a new acquaintance then proceeding to précis my whole life in an afternoon's chat. It was a lot of time to catch up on.

I left them, found my swimming trunks and headed down towards the beach. It was another black sandy strip, and the sea was inky. It led into the water at a sharp angle, and in just a few steps the waves were up to my neck. I struck out in slight trepidation at the enormous depth below me. As I swam, the volcano roared. It was an alien noise, a sound effect belonging to a movie or sci-fi machinery; it was unlike anything I'd ever heard before. It gave out an astounding sensation, too, because it was forged at such a low frequency. Without doubt, it was the deepest sound I had ever felt. It made me tingle. It was thrilling: it was nature at its surround-sound stereophonic best. I floated, wanting the mountain to bellow again. Something was happening to me. Since when the fascination with nature? I had already narrowly escaped turning into a hippie. I had to keep myself in check: I could feel a serious case of bucolia coming on.

I trekked back to Maria's the long way round, retracing some of the dirt tracks that I'd already paraded along courtesy of the tractor. I skirted the main village and turned back towards the house. I arrived late in the afternoon to find Maria alone in the dark house.

'I told Eva to rest,' she said. 'I still want to get a doctor.'

'You know, doctors aren't what it's all about, Maria. She's doing it her way – she's done it her way all along. It's too late for her to turn back now. Support her. She needs it.'

'Of course I do, Jake. But what about me? I'm an old woman, and I don't think I can look after her.' Maria looked lost. Suddenly I felt like a guardian or a parent. The roles were reversing and I had to take care of the two older women.

'Nobody's asked you to look after her, Maria. I'm doing that.' I was no longer on holiday taking each opportunity as it came. I was there because I wanted to be.

'Eva was about your age when I first met her. Do you know how beautiful my angel was then? She is special, Jake.'

'I can tell she was beautiful.'

'I thought I would never lose her. When she came into my

life, it was like she cast a spell. It would only be summer with Eva and Goose.'

Maria had tripped back in time; she changed visibly as her memories tumbled back.

'She spent nearly a year with me. It was perfect, Jake. I loved that girl like she was my own daughter, and when she left the island she said it would only be for a short time. It has taken so long for my baby to return. I don't think you know what it's like to lose someone like that.'

She was right, I didn't.

I found Eva lying on one of the beds. It was the first time I'd seen her use a bed. She was looking fed up. 'Maybe this isn't right,' she said.

'What's the problem now?'

'It's Maria, I'm not so sure she cares about me. Not me as Eva. I think she only sees a middle-aged woman with cancer.'

Eva had described herself as someone I didn't recognise. Who was this sick middle-aged woman? It wasn't the person I knew now.

'I don't think that's the case, y'know. She worries because she loves you. Of course she fucking cares. Would you take in someone you hadn't seen for twenty years when they show up out of the blue with a strange queen floating along in tow? I mean, what did you expect, Eva?'

It was as if she needed discord to survive. She was fighting again, but this time she was not attacking her cancer on the inside: she'd altered her focus. She was trying to hurt the outside.

'All she sees is cancer.'

'She can't get her head around it, that's all. Christ, it's taken me a while to get friendly with your growth and I've been with you solidly for the last month. You know what? Maybe Maria is wrestling with her own notions of death. I'm not so sure that she's able to take on someone else's life-threatening dramas.'

I felt terrible. I'd acknowledged Eva's illness as being mortal. I'd subconsciously bought into the finality of it. It came as a shock: the two of us sat on our respective beds thinking about the words that had carelessly stumbled out. Neither of us spoke: we had traversed a boundary that should never have been crossed. I had stepped out of place. But any notions of fate were soon banished.

'Why don't we go out, Jake? It's time for me to show you my favourite place in the whole wide world.'

We set out from the house and slowly climbed a track towards the base of the volcano. Eva was sluggish, and she was wheezing more than she had before. She was disguising her difficulty, I could see: she wanted me to believe she was enjoying the walk and only stopping to admire the view. I knew better. It was still just light, but by the time we reached the meadow the sun had all but gone, the long grass was no more than a hazy silhouette in the twilight and the crater above us glowed red in the fast-approaching darkness.

'Yeah, fabulous, Eva. Gorgeous view, not. I think we'll save this one for another day.'

'Let's just stay awhile, Jake.'

We sat down in the grass. Eva was breathing deeply and slowly. It was like she was sucking in secrets from the air around us.

'Let's come back here in daylight, Eva. C'mon, let's go back to the house.'

She didn't want to move. She wanted to become part of the ground and stay hidden in the long grass.

'Come on, it's too dark now.'

I persuaded her to leave the hill and her ghosts to make our protracted return to Maria's place.

While we were out Maria had been in the kitchen, where she had conjured up not only food but an atmosphere of celebration. She was happy: the smells of cooking were mixed with sounds of her pleasure, she was sizzling, gurgling, almost singing the food to the table. Her frying and boiling had baked away the strangeness of earlier and filled the house with a new purpose. It was a simple feast, sumptuous to look at and ravishing to eat. The local wine was nectar. Maria was in her element: she'd obviously been created by the local gods to cook for and feed others.

Afterwards we went to our room and something strange happened: Eva didn't bother with the origami – she got into the bed. Neither of us mentioned it.

'If you're going to use the shower, Jake, can you do it when I'm not about?'

'Sure, in the morning, maybe.'

The obsessions had disappeared.

STROMBOLI

There is something Baroque and twisted about the village on Stromboli, something lonely and distorted. It is Catholic and blackly religious. Like a parasite in a troublesome partnership, it holds desperately to the furthest point of its big angry host. It's a nervous parish. The atmosphere there was distinctive, more oblique than that on Vulcano. Yet again Eva and I had become objects of curiosity, but this time it was from far off. It wasn't overt; it was simultaneously camouflaged yet omnipresent. People peeped at us then turned away. Maybe we were protected there by Maria's standing in the community, shielded by our friendship with her. I still felt like a Z-list celebrity in a supermarket, though. In the centre of the village was an impressive church just crying out for a good old-fashioned Mafia funeral and a few shops. In the evening everything lit up like a carnival and the tiny streets swarmed with life, not that I believed many people lived there. I was under the distinct impression that everybody doubled and tripled up, like a low-budget movie. A gang of kids, for instance, might promenade down the street once, belt home, get changed then do it all over again, just to make the populace look bigger than it was.

It was our second night in Seismic Central and Eva and I wandered into the village, leaving Maria in a cooking frenzy. We sat outside an ancient café, Eva with a glass of hot water and one of the last of her evil herbal brews, me with a glass of wine and a fag. It was then that I developed my theory on the expanding population. It seemed to be working a treat until a new face buggered up my theory.

'Hello. You must be Jake.'

I was completely taken aback.

'I'm sorry?'

'You must be Jake. My name's Toni. I'm Alessandro's friend. Have you seen him?'

Toni seemed to stretch on for ever. He was long and lean with a very round head thatched with white-grey hair. He looked like a pin.

'I saw him a few days ago on Vulcano, Toni. You know his hotel has closed for the season? I don't know what he's doing now.'

Our micro-celebrity had reached much further afield than the sulphuric confines of Vulcano.

'Oh, I know that – he's here somewhere with me. We've lost each other.'

Alessandro was making a bid for freedom from the Casa Becci with the help of a prosperous prick and a luxury yacht.

'We're cruising to Napoli, but I wanted to stop off here for the volcano. It's wonderful, isn't it?'

Toni's head might have been attached to his skinny frame with rubber bands: it bounced and rocked from side to side in a perversely endearing way.

'This is Eva.'

'I know. Very nice to meet you, Signora.'

He was standing over our table looking lost.

'Do you want to join us, Toni?'

'That is very kind. Thank you.'

So, this was Alessandro's special friend, his new mate. I couldn't imagine why Toni should know anything of me. Perhaps Alessandro chanced his luck with everyone who passed through Vulcano, so the odds of a mutual acquaintanceship, no matter how nebulous, were pretty high.

'How did you know who we were?'

'Alessandro pointed you out to me, he's told me all about you. Everybody knows everyone else on the islands. He tells me you're a bit of a high flier in the design world.'

I smiled awkwardly, and Eva smirked into her tea. 'I'm not quite so skyscraping. I think Alessandro has got a hold of the wrong end of the stick.'

'You're very modest, Jake. I'm sure Alessandro would love you both to join us on the boat for dinner. I know I would. Can I persuade you?'

For a split second I was tempted. I rather liked the idea of seeing a gay gin palace – *and* Alessandro's face when he found us there. But Eva was staring at me. She'd guessed what I was thinking and didn't like (what she imagined to be) the look I was giving Toni. 'That's kind of you, Toni,' she said, 'but Jake and I have another supper engagement. I'm sorry. I think it's time we went back to Maria's now.'

'Will she be ready for us, Eva?'

'*Ja*. Let's go.'

Eva started off down the street. I left a few coins on the

table and got up to follow her. 'Toni, I'm sorry, I have to go. Maybe another day?'

'Don't worry. I'm here for a while yet. Enjoy your supper tonight. It was nice meeting you.'

By the time I caught up with Eva she had already reached the church, which surprised me. 'That was a quick exit, Eva, are you OK?'

'*Ja*. I'm fine.'

'You could have fooled me. What's wrong?'

'Nothing.'

Eva was looking heated and directional. She was like a dog pulling at a leash.

'Is this a bit of the old green eye?'

She ignored me.

'It is. You're peeved because I showed an interest in Toni and his yacht, aren't you?'

'No, of course not.'

'Eva, it wasn't even a flirtation. For God's sake, nothing has happened. I'm not going to stow away with him to Naples on the Good Ship *Lollipop*. I'm staying here. With you.'

It was true: I was with Eva. We carried on walking. There was nowhere else that I wanted to be; we could stay on the island for ever.

'I'm sorry, I was being silly, Jake. I did feel jealous for a moment, I couldn't help it. I know you won't run away from me.'

We walked away arm in arm from the sparkling lights of the village into the darkness of the track that led back to Maria's.

'Eva, you do know that no matter how much I want to I

can't stay much longer? We'll both have to think of going back to London soon, or at least I will.'

'I suppose so. When will you be going?'

'Won't we both go?'

'*Ja*, *Ja*, of course we shall. Let's figure that out later. Let's go home now. I'm getting very tired.'

We aimed back to the house. Aromatic smells drifted out of the kitchen. When we went in, Maria turned from the stove. 'You're back in time. I make something special for you. To make you well, Eva.'

I wondered whether Maria had been cooking or casting spells – it didn't matter because it smelt great.

'You eat this and I make you better, you see. No more cancer. We send the cancer to Calabria. Go on, you cancer, go and join the witch in Calabria.'

It didn't matter that the food had a voodoo pedigree; it was delicious.

GOOSE

The morning light in the bedroom was a revelation. It was exceptional, snappy and technicolour: the sky had never been so blue. This was the morning on which Eva was going to show me her meadow. We set off up the track again, headed towards the foot of the volcano and found the other night's spot. We sat down in long grass littered with wild flowers and listened to the cataclysmic growling from the volcano behind us. Eva started to tell me about her last visit to the island all those years before.

Nineteen sixty-nine was the year in which her life had changed. She'd come to Stromboli with her fella, Gustaf, and decided to hang out on the island. It was hippie shit, she was young and prettily handsome, Gustaf was a beautiful boy-babe and they'd fallen deeply in love. 'I used to listen to the radio, tight against my ear, with my eyes shut, and all I could see was pink. It was beautiful, Jake. I can see it now. Gustaf would lie down just here, all brown and naked and stoned. Do you ever smoke?'

I was looking at the clouds and the blue, blue sky that Gustaf had been peering into twenty years ago. 'I don't think I need a joint right now, Eva.'

'I don't know why I had a radio, I never really knew what I was listening to. I always thought those days would last for ever. I had a beautiful white kaftan embroidered all around the neck and I had a long piece of bright pink Indian silk that I tied my hair up in.'

As Eva spoke a barely perceptible breeze caught and rearranged her chiffon scarves.

'It makes me laugh now.'

'What?'

'Gustaf. He was so pretty, all long curly hair and a little boy's body.'

I tried to capture the two of them – I could see Eva better than I could see him, with clean fresh skin. She was exquisite, a golden girl.

'Maria always said the witch had cast a spell on him – she said the naughty witch who lives in Calabria made him sleep. He did sleep an awful lot. We built a boat once out of old planks and rope. Shall we look for it?'

We didn't move: we just looked out to the horizon hoping to catch a glimpse of Gustaf waving back from his homemade skiff.

'I called him Goose, Jake . . . he called me H.'

'H?'

'It didn't mean anything, it was just his nickname for me.'

I was told a fairy-tale. They had painted pictures and built boats, they'd hidden away on the island with a transistor radio and a bag of dope. The witch had thrown a sleepy spell; the two of them had done that whole hippie thing of tuning in and dropping out. Their life was perfect. Eva had befriended Maria, who had in turn become a mother, Eva's mother.

'Where's your real mother, Eva?'

Eva leant back into the grass and shut her eyes.

'Is she still alive?'

'*Ja*. I suppose so.'

'You don't know? Don't you ever speak?'

She tightened her eyes, screwing them right up.

'What's the problem between you?'

'Do you know, Jake, the awful thing is that I can't remember what the problem is? I've been out of her life for so long now that I don't know her, don't need her. I don't even think about her. This is the first time I've spoken about her in years.'

I didn't believe her. 'That's bollocks, Eva.'

'What?'

'Of course you know why you haven't spoken. She's not another person you've mislaid somewhere in time.' Then it occurred to me that perhaps I was digging too deep. What had gone on between Eva and her mother was none of my bloody business. 'So why the rift, then?'

Eva looked away from me. 'A long time ago, a very long time ago, my mother wanted me to have an abortion. She thought I should get rid of a . . . "socially undesirable baby". Those were her words. Can you imagine a baby, my baby – any baby – being "socially undesirable"?'

I hugged my knees.

'It was Gustaf's baby, if you must know. I was so stupid, Jake, I let it happen. I let her take it away from me. It was such a terrible, awful time. I had a breakdown. I couldn't cope. I stayed in Munich for another few months and couldn't bear it any longer. I ran off here with Goose.'

I had dug too deep. Eva looked weepy.

'And you know what? After all the heartbreak and running away, the bastard ran out on me. I had my soul pulled out of me that year.'

Her little bit of heaven had shattered along the way. But while it had lasted this was where it had been.

'And I can't stop blaming my mother for all that shit, for all my unhappiness. You really think I want to speak with her? She's dead, Jake, my family and my baby. I killed them twenty years ago.'

The volcano guttered and Eva let out a tiny sob. I put my arm around her tiny, fragile, bony shoulder and held on while she cried silently. I felt as if I was her dead child, her runaway lover, her new parent.

OPPORTUNITY

At the back of Maria's house was a large and spiteful pomegranate tree. It dominated the terrace that led upwards from the courtyard towards the volcano, a pincushion laden with fruit. I was voted in by an overwhelming majority of two to become pomegranate picker for the sick and the elderly, and was shunted up a rickety ladder. It was the first time in years that anything had been picked from the antique tree. The pomegranates were bright red and bursting, sweet and delicious. I scratched myself getting to them, but my blood looked duller than the juice that spattered my white linen shorts. Lunch was salami, cheese and olives – we'd eat the fruit later. I was buying into the luxey life of peasant chic and could feel myself revving up for an intense session with an Italian Elizabeth David, pottery crockery and a fistful of herbs. It was seductive.

Maria went back inside – she was plotting more food for the evening – and left Eva and me to play in the shade of the tree. Eva had got hold of a pile of paper and spread it out in front of her. She started scribbling, drawing quirky stick-men and birds with long tails. Her images were stark and slightly sinister. She drew a dog with pinprick eyes and especially sharp teeth; it was black and dangerous-looking and hid ominously in the corner of the page.

'Here, Jake, time to draw me a picture. Go on. I want something to remember this beautiful day by.'

She handed me a large curly piece of paper. It was difficult to flatten it out on the ground. I didn't really know what to draw, so I flicked red ink over the page absentmindedly and rubbed it into the paper.

'It looks like a massacre.'

'It's my pomegranate picture. There – does that look better?' I had drawn a few branches.

'It still looks like a bloodbath to me. Why don't you do this, Jakey?' Eva added little green flashes. 'You see? It's beginning to look like a tree now.'

I looked at the doodle Eva had come up with; the dog was still ready to attack. I thought he needed a bone. 'Do you mind if I feed that mutt, Eva?'

Gradually we started to add to each other's sketches. Drawing together and scratching patterns into the dust on the terrace. We suspended coloured scraps of paper around us, decorating the plants with fake new leaves. The yard was looking like a whimsical jewellery box. We had subconsciously re-created our own version of twenty years before. We'd become eighties hippies trying to escape my return to London and Eva's reality. We were trying to escape an ancient abortion and a profligate life punctuated with nightclubs and cocaine. We were trying to lose any number of demons that scratched away at us. We were trying to exorcise the thing that was gnawing away from inside out: Eva's cancer. The two of us had been running from that ever since we had met a month earlier at the Alitalia desk.

Reality check fourteen: 'You know Eva, I have to go home soon.'

I had broken the magic.

'Stay for another few days.'

'I don't think I can.'

'You could stay till the end of next week. Then we could travel back to London together.'

I had to think of my other life. 'It's not going to work. I have to get back to my flat and sort out the shit that's bound to be waiting there for me. And I've got to go to work . . . Or find myself another job.'

Eva looked deflated. 'Go on, stay for just another week.'

'I can't. I'd love to but, Eva, I've been away so much longer than I thought. Why don't you come back with me a little earlier?'

It was obvious that she wouldn't or couldn't: she was set to stay those extra days on Stromboli. She needed to stay as much as I needed to go home.

'You do understand, Eva? I have to go back.'

'Yes. Of course. Do you have enough money for your fare to London?'

'You *are* kidding me, Eva?'

'Then we'll have to ask Richard to organise a ticket for you. I'll sort out the money with him when I get back. Go on, you'd better get started. Go and call him, sort out your ticket.'

She looked resigned to my departure, but saddened. I left her surrounded by paintings and alien plants with painted leaves. As I walked past the kitchen I could hear Maria muttering something about Calabria as she prepared the evening meal.

Toni and Alessandro came promenading down the street towards me.

'Jake, where are you off to?'

'I'm trying to find the phone.'

'Let me show you the way,' Toni said. 'It's up here. I'm pleased I've seen you. We're leaving the island later.'

'You are?'

'Yes, Alessandro is anxious to move on, aren't you? Napoli next and then Roma.'

'That's just what I'm trying to do. It's time for me to go.'

'Will you join us for coffee after you telephone?'

'Sure.'

'Hey, Dick, it's Jake.'

'Where are you?'

'Don't start.'

'What do you mean, "don't start"? What the hell are you doing, Jake?'

'Can you get me a ticket home?'

'You're coming back?'

'Yeah. Get me a flight. Rome airport will be as good as any.'

'You want me to sort this out for you?'

'Yes, please. And could you meet me at Heathrow?'

'Heathrow?'

'You've got to, I don't have any money to get home with.'

'Fine, I'll sort it out for you. Will Eva will be coming too?'

'Nope, she's staying on for another few days. She'll be back next week.'

I didn't want to speak about Eva for fear of a row, but I couldn't help it. 'Dick, I think you have a lot of talking to do.'

'Don't get involved in my private life, Jake. This has nothing to do with you.'

I was right. He was getting cantankerous.

'I'll get your ticket, can you call me later for the details?'

'Of course I will. Thank you. I'll call you tomorrow. 'Bye.'

Toni, Alessandro and I went to the coffee shop.

'If you're going to Roma, Jake, why don't you join us? We should be there in two days.'

'Thanks, Toni, but I'll make my own way.'

'Come with us today, it'll be great fun.'

'No, thank you, I can't. It's very kind of you to offer, but I'm staying with Maria tonight.'

I had no need of new opportunities. I felt a detached empathy with Alessandro: he was running away, he'd grabbed his chance, like I had a hundred times before. But he was fleeing into the unknown and I was going home. Both of us would have to fight to survive. It was a strange camaraderie.

I walked back to Maria's place, kicking up a trail of dust as I went. Her kitchen was home to more of her sorcery. On the big planky table was a huge steaming bowl of *spaghetti alle vongole* to which we helped ourselves.

'Look at my hands, Jake, I can't get the paint off them.'

Eva's hands had a tracery of indigo dye all over them, as if the veins had come to the surface. She didn't ask about Richard or the ticket, so we carried on as if nothing would change. We weren't running any more: we were grappling with our new world.

FEAR

Maria had been up for ever. She had been baking bread and had brought some, along with coffee, to the room. I took the tray from her and sat down on my bed, slowly waking up with those delicious early-morning smells. After eating our indoor picnic Eva and I stayed in our room later than usual. There was a curiousness between us: it wasn't an unpleasant feeling, just a frisson I hadn't felt before. It was a barely perceivable difference and it felt quite nice. We were getting arty again. There were more paintings and drawings and lazy conversation. We were contented and affectionate with each other.

'Are you going to paint all day or are you going to call Dick at some point?' she asked me.

I carried on doodling.

'You need to find out about your ticket, don't you, Jake?'

'Yeah, I'll go in a min.' I felt safe and complacent; the idea of leaving the bedroom was too much.

'Jake, c'mon, get your act together. If you go now we'll have the rest of the day together.'

I was apprehensive. I didn't want to find out that I was definitely leaving: I wanted to remain in our reconstructed fantasy, painting pictures. Heck, we might even build a boat.

'Jake! Don't prevaricate – go, will you?'

I sloped off to find the telephone and returned twenty minutes later. 'Eva? It's done. I'm flying back the day after tomorrow.'

'That's wonderful, so we've still got another full day together on the island.'

'Wrong, I have to leave first thing tomorrow on the Aliscafi. I have to get myself to Rome for the lunchtime flight the next day.'

I felt a little nauseous. Fuck, what was it? The flight confirmation had left me in a state approaching depression. It was the realisation that I was definitely leaving. Today, this afternoon and this evening, were the last few hours I would spend on Stromboli.

'What's the matter with you two, then?' Maria had appeared at the door. 'I've not seen you all day. Are you ill, Eva?'

'No, I'm fine. I'm sad because Jake's flying back to London. He's got to leave tomorrow.'

'Don't worry, you go after him next week. You're not staying here for ever.'

Eva gave Maria one of her more acidic stares.

'But you don't stay, Eva. You say you go after Jake in a few days.'

'I know. I'll be leaving on Wednesday or Thursday. It's not that that's upsetting me.'

'Then what is it?'

'Change, Maria. Nothing stays as it should, does it? We get everything so perfect and then it goes again. I'm tired of it. I want something to remain for once. I want life to be good.'

A one-way ticket to London had filleted the rural idyll in the middle-class peasant's bijou abode.

'It worries me – how can I look after you when Jake's gone?'

'There's nothing for you to do, Maria. We've been over this before, haven't we? There is nothing to worry about. I'll be fine. And then I'll be gone back to London before you realise it.'

'That's not what I want you to do.'

'Then what is it?'

Maria started to smooth her apron as she had when she was first told about Eva's cancer. 'I'm scared.'

I was startled by that. 'Scared' was the one feeling that hadn't manifested itself in me. Desolation, hysteria at a push, but I had never been scared. I looked at Eva. Was she scared? I'd never thought about it. I'd always believed she was in control. I couldn't see behind her gaunt face. What was I looking for? There was nothing for her to be scared about. Our trip was nearly over, she'd be safely back in London soon.

'You don't understand. I'm not afraid of the cancer, I'm afraid for us.'

Maria chilled the room as if she had thrown one of the Calabrian witch's premonitions at us.

I butted in nervously: 'Maria, don't be silly. Nothing's going to happen after I've gone. Does it look like Eva's going to be ill? No, of course not. Now, I don't want to be quarrelling on my last day.'

'I worry for us all, Jake – you, Eva and me. I don't want to lose you again. What are we going to do?'

'We're going to get on with living, Maria, like Eva and I are going to get on with our drawing.'

I was lying. Maria had sewn a fragment of her insecurity into me. Her fear had become mine. I wanted to start running again or take cover beneath her apron. I would do anything to escape the old woman's intuition. Maria walked back to her kitchen, set on plunging herself into a baking fury. More bread, two cakes. She was going to cook her way out of despondency and despair. She might even find a spell to ensnare the runaways.

Eva picked up three of the largest drawings and started folding them carefully.

'What are you doing with those?' I asked.

'We've not made a boat yet. Let's go sailing.'

We limped to the beach and crossed the gritty black sand to the water. We'd become phantoms again, white spooks in a black landscape. There was no one there apart from us and I felt terribly lonely.

'Here, Jake, one for you, one for me, and here's one for . . . whoever.'

We paddled a little way into the sea and launched the colourful paper boats. They headed out, bobbing across the water. Mine sank after coming undone, but Eva's and whoever's went a little further before being sucked into the blackness by a wave. We walked back up the shore and sat on a rock. Eva was half humming and half murmuring; her song sounded like a call to prayer. I stripped down to my trunks and lazed next to her in the sleepy heat. Time had stretched again and we lost the afternoon.

'C'mon, Eva, let's go and find Maria before she's cooked enough for the five thousand.'

The night-time was hot and syrupy. It had never been quite so overpowering during our stay on Stromboli. We ate the evening meal under the pomegranate tree and Maria pulled out a couple of extra-special bottles of red wine for the occasion. 'Let's drink these. We celebrate your last night on Stromboli, Jake.'

'You don't need to, Maria, save them for a proper occasion.'

'Don't be silly, there's no one else for me to serve them to. Go on, drink up, Jake.'

There was really only one person she was serving the wine to that night, because Eva and she had just a small glass each.

Maria had created a feast: fresh sardines with lemon, her delish bread, porcini risotto with the best Parmesan, zucchini and spinach squashy with oil. There was a bean salad and salad leaves, and a dessert of some sort in the fridge as well as a cake. There was way too much food – we'd been too late to prevent our inverted witch from producing a chaotic miracle. The wine remained alcoholic; her wizardry didn't stretch to conversion.

The morning's prophecy had been forgotten. Or, at least, it wasn't referred to. No, the only vibe this evening was one that had been building up inside me. It was the opposite to the strangeness at the beginning of the day. I was feeling hurt but was unable to express it; I was imprisoned by an unfamiliar gut reaction. My mental swirl was straining and the stitches were pulling: I was fit to burst. There was more silence than conversation, and it was broken by a roar from the volcano, a sound that had sucked itself from the centre of the world. It was as if the mountain had exploded for me.

We all looked up. Maria seemed even more surprised than we were. 'I think you two have woken up my hill,' she said. She tut-tutted, then started to clear the table. 'No, stop it, Eva, and you, Jake. I'll do this. You two stay out here, enjoy the evening.'

When Maria had gone in, the mountain bellowed again.

'It's amazing, Jake. I don't remember the volcano ever being that loud.'

'I guess it's a farewell holler, Eva. Imagine what it'll do when you leave next week. You'll probably get fireworks as well.'

Eva smiled. She, like me, was thinking back to our first night and the pyrotechnics we had watched on Vulcano.

Eventually Maria came back from the kitchen. 'I'm off to bed now, my dears. Everything's cleared. I'll leave you two love birds alone. See you in the morning.'

Eva and I looked at each other. I reached for my glass; I needed to shift the attention. Maria knew more about Eva and me than we did.

'I'm going to miss you, Jake, when you've gone.'

'You'll be back in London next week. It's only a few days.'

The rim of the crater was intensely red. I imagined I could see flames pricking the black sky.

'I'll still miss you, Jake.'

'You know what? I'll miss you too.'

Eva had her elbow on the table and started to chew her fingertips. In the dim light she looked like an African mask with a long thick tongue stretching down to the tabletop. She breathed in so deeply it was as if she was hoping the air would keep anything she wanted to say securely tucked inside her.

Eventually she broke the quiet. 'Jake, will you meet me off the plane when I get back next week?'

'Yes, of course.'

'You won't run away from me, will you?'

'No. Don't be silly. I'm not going to run anywhere.'

I lit another cigarette and poured some more wine into my glass. I could feel tears coming up from my chest. I wasn't going to cry. 'I can't believe I'm going without you,' I said. I spoke on an inhalation and my voice was a little too high. 'It's strange. I can't imagine London. I want to stay here with you and Maria.'

Eva put her hand on mine and squeezed. She was holding on to the moment. 'Jake, let's go to bed.'

We left my half-empty glass under the tree and went to our room. I could see Eva's silhouette against the window: she was nothing but a ripple in the sheets. 'Eva, you're a wonderful friend.'

'You're not so bad yourself.'

I lay awake, looking at the ceiling, waiting for sleep to catch me. 'Eva, I love you.'

There was no reply, I didn't know if she had heard me or not. I pushed my face into the pillow and fell asleep to the mutterings of the mountain.

The next morning's light seemed even more crystalline and stringent than before. Eva was already up and I threw my clothes into my knackered case, found some tape and tried to repair it for my journey home. In the kitchen Maria had the coffee on and Eva was sitting at the table.

'You'll write to me, won't you, Jake? You won't forget your new friend on Stromboli, will you?' said Maria.

'Of course I'll write. Heck, I'll probably be back here to stay again, if you'll have me.'

'You're always welcome. You know you both can always stay with me.'

I looked over to Eva. She was doing one of her half-completed smiles. It didn't have a beginning or an end. 'I've gotta make a move, H, or I'll miss the boat.'

Eva blinked at me. 'Are you calling me H now?'

I had flipped her back in time. 'It slipped out.'

'That's fine. I like it.'

She reached over and touched the sleeve of my shirt, as if she were about to straighten it or pick off a fleck. 'Come on, Jake, I'll see you to the door.'

The three of us stood on the step in the impossible sunlight.

'Don't forget to write, Jake.' Maria almost bent forward when she spoke, as if she was talking to a child.

'Of course I won't.'

'You don't forget your new friend Maria.'

'I promise – how could I?'

'I've made this for you, something to eat on your journey.' She handed over a carrier-bag packed with enough sandwiches to feed a family.

Eva stood behind her. Her eyes were smarting. 'See you next week, Jake. I'm not good at goodbyes.'

Maria was being used as a shield.

'Let me know when your flight is. I'll be there to meet you.'

'I'll call you. Now move on, Jake, don't miss the ferry.'

Maria and Eva turned to go back inside and I started to walk down the lane. I broke into a run, clutching my case hard against my chest and found myself weeping.

BACK TO REALITY

The Aliscafi was already sitting in the harbour, the engines throbbing. As I sat down it sped off, as if it was desperate to race away from Stromboli. I felt empty; I was a husk. The air-con felt cold so I sat by the window to catch the sun and watch as the island was dragged into the distance. The spray kicked up by the boat was spitting at the volcano. I started to eat one of Maria's sandwiches, to feel better rather than because I was hungry. I kept trying to see the island, but it got smaller and smaller, and within a few minutes had all but gone. As we headed for Naples the water became flat and we sliced our way past other boats. Perhaps one had Toni and Alessandro aboard. That didn't distract me, though, from imagining that a tiny smudge on the horizon might still be Stromboli. It wasn't, it had vanished. I felt as if a great big chunk of my life had been taken away. It had, temporarily. I was in love.

After what seemed like no time Naples came whizzing into view. I sat and watched the other passengers rounding up their bags and children, and pushing to the front of the boat, then started to look around me. Something was missing – Eva's luggage. I wasn't sure that she'd manage by herself when she made the same trip in a week's time. She could leave the bloody juicer with Maria. She could leave it all with Maria, then she'd have stuff ready for her when we went back. Surely we would return.

The boat docked and I walked out into the hot Neapolitan sunshine – I'd forgotten how hot it was after the chill in the cabin. I found a café, lit a ciggy and downed a coffee. Gradually I was beginning to feel like another me. It was the person I'd been before I'd met a strange woman in the airport. My days on the islands had started to peel off. I was fretting and still thinking about Eva, but somehow the Aeolian dream was losing its grip. I found a copy of *The Times* abandoned on the next table; it was a few days out of date. I was becoming part of the other world again. Fuck; get a grip.

Life awareness: hello. Eva would be back in London in a week, what was the big deal? It was time to get back into gear, gee myself up and get my arse back home. I walked to the station and bought a ticket, jumped aboard a train and bolted towards Rome. It was like watching a movie at the wrong speed: villages and towns whipped into view and away again, trees barely made a flash as the express hurled itself northwards. I could feel a fragile excitement tingling inside me, the same shiver I'd experienced when I landed in Palermo. I arrived in the capital: this was not going to be easy because I had virtually no money. A tout sidled up with the offer of a hotel I could afford but I made one stipulation: 'I don't give a shit about anything but this place had better have a bath and hot water.'

'What you mean? I no give you bad hotel. It's a good hotel. A family hotel.'

He gave me a disgusted look that barely registered from beneath his eyelids. Not that a look was going to worry me. I'd done looks – Palermo looks, Messina looks, Vulcano and Stromboli looks. My Roman friend had a lot of competition if he was going to make his mark in the scrutinisation stakes. Reassured of hot water, a tub and the cheapest deal in town, I followed the guy through the narrow, noisy, fume-filled streets. It was my first taste of city in a while; I didn't know if I liked it.

La Perla was a hotel with no frontage, a door wedged between other doors. We went in, and walked along a narrow, claustrophobic corridor decorated with crappy tourist posters of the islands. At the end of the hall was a tiny reception that barely accommodated the round man sitting at the desk. I wanted to see Karin and the Contessa. I wanted Isabella and the grannies. I wanted Maria. I wanted Eva.

'How many nights?'

'One.'

'Passport. *Grazie.* You have room seventeen. Go up the stairs to the top floor and go to the end of the hall. Enjoy your stay, Mr . . . Mr Jones.'

I didn't hold out great hopes for a wonderful time, but that didn't matter – the only thing that counted right at that moment was a bath. A long, hot, comfortable bath. I found my sad little room and across the hall was a cheerless bathroom. I didn't give a shit. I could clean myself properly for the first time in weeks. I tried to open the louvred shutters but they were jammed. I pushed hard and eventually they gave way to the filthiest courtyard in Rome. It was an abject, desolate slum. It seemed every window in the surrounding buildings had been opened in an effort to escape the last of the day's heat, and from every one came the cacophonous sound of disagreement, disembodied voices and crazed TVs. Any number of radios were in on the act too. It felt like hell. I closed the shutters and looked at the bath. I turned on the tap and brown sludge trickled out. I tried the light, it popped. I understood that Michelangelo had installed the plumbing and Leonardo had obviously had a hand in the electrics. Neither had been looked at since. The fragile excitement abated and dementia took over. I ran downstairs, a maddened harridan screaming for blood and hot water and wiring that didn't have medieval provenance.

'What's the matter? You don't like my hotel?'

The hotelier was giving me one of the tout's looks.

'Just give me a bath, a clean fucking bath, and then I'll be happy. Then I'll love your hotel. Just let me clean myself.'

A mixture of trepidation and pity took hold of the man and he let me use his own bathroom. 'Will you be OK now?'

'Yes, thank you. This is all I need.'

I could tell he thought I was insane. He edged out of the room and I locked the door. I luxuriated in hot water for the first time in weeks. I looked along the shelves – guessed he had daughters as he obviously didn't have a feminine side of his own – and poured the best part of a bottle of bubble bath into the water. Fuck, it felt good. I stayed in there, silently, for a couple of hours, until the bloke crept back and knocked gingerly on the door to assess my progress. Perhaps he thought I'd topped myself with a bottle of his aspirin and one of his razors. I got out of the tub feeling improbably revived, headed upstairs for a quick change and then out.

I had stepped into someone else's sphere. I was a stranger. I had no interest in what was around me. I was walking along in my own little world post-Eva, post-everything. I was a Space Cadet without the drugs. I found a pizza joint and sat down at a table on the pavement, but this time there were no laughs with the local boys, no flirtations or boozy assignations. There were no bullfights with Coke cans, no gurnings from Eva. I'd had enough of everything and headed straight back to the hotel, climbed the stairs and fell into the deepest sleep.

I awoke with no idea of the time and somebody knocking at the door. It was a chambermaid. ***Reality check fifteen***: that could mean only one thing – it must be midday. I tore downstairs, settled the bill and raced on to the street in search of a cab. It was twelve thirty. I had just enough money to get me to the airport and not quite enough time to get me there. We made a dash for it anyway. Every red light was ignored and we under- and overtook. The heat had put me in a trance. It didn't matter that I was tossed from one side of the vehicle to the other: I couldn't feel it. My sleepiness meant that the city had disappeared before I'd even seen it. We drove along the motorway and eventually swung towards the airport. I paid the driver all the money I had and ran into the building. It was cool again, but my shirt was sticking to my back. I ran past the cops – they were armed with machine-guns and strutting their sexy leather-clad stuff by the departure gate – and found the BA desk.

'You're very late. Ticket, please.'

'I don't have one. I have to collect it from here.'

'There's nothing I can do without a ticket.'

'I am to collect it from here.'

The trolley dolly from hell had been retired from the heavens to rule *terra firma* with attitude. He looked bored and pinched; everything was too much hassle for him. I didn't know how to react. Four weeks ago I'd have yelled; 'Find my frigging ticket or I promise you you'll have a grubby encounter with a messed-up queen to deal with.' I'd have fucked with him harder than he could fuck with me. But I didn't, I just stood and stared.

The ticket clerk went off to consult with his manageress who, in turn, looked up at me over imaginary bifocals. 'What seems to be the problem?'

'All I want is my ticket.'

'Name?'

'Jones – Mr J. Jones.'

'Here we go. You don't have very much time. Better keep your case with you – you'll have to run to gate twenty-seven.'

She looked at me carefully. I still wasn't moving. 'Run and get your plane. Have a good trip.'

I ricocheted from passport control and security to my gate, and was the last to board the flight. My case didn't have too much life left in it. The Sellotape was starting to go and I was trailing chiffon. I found my seat and sank as far back as it was possible to go in cattle-class. I didn't even notice when we took off.

Later I was given a piddly bag of peanuts and proceeded

to do gentle damage to a few miniatures of vodka and tonic. I was going home. It was as if I were on rewind.

HOME

Heathrow. I looked about for Richard – he wasn't there, so I walked up and down Arrivals feeling pissed off. I didn't want to hang around. Eventually I hung out at the end of the queue of banner-waving cabbies and waited.

'Excuse me, are you Jake?' A tall blonde girl was staring at me. She had a ruddy face, as if she had been running.

'Yes. I'm sorry, you are?'

'Hi, I'm Yasmin, Richard asked me to find you. Sorry I'm a bit late – you know what it's like, bloody tubes. Here, I've got something for you.' She handed me an envelope. 'It's like we're spies, isn't it? Here's your assignment, Jake, be sure to eat the contents after you've read them.' She was smiling.

'Where's Richard then?'

'Oh, he's busy. He says hi and glad you're back and he'll see you on Monday at the studio.'

I opened the envelope. Inside was twenty quid.

'I've already got a return ticket for the tube, Jake. Are you going to travel back with me?'

'Yeah, sure. I'll just pay my fare . . .'

We sat side by side not saying very much to begin with.

'Richard tells me you've been in Italy,' she began.

'Yeah.'

'You've got a great tan. Did you have a nice time?'

'I suppose I did. In the end, thank you.'

'Richard and I were thinking of going to Italy. Whereabouts did you go?'

'The islands. Just off Sicily.'

Did I hear that properly? 'You say you and Richard are going to Italy?'

'Yes. He's been so stressed out recently, we thought a holiday away from it all would be the answer.'

I was shocked.

'Yes, not sure where we're going yet. I was hoping you'd be able to recommend somewhere nice.'

The train had come out of the tunnel and was zipping past the suburbs towards central London. There wasn't any sunlight. I didn't know if I wanted to be sitting with Yasmin.

'Have you known him long?' I asked.

'We've been going out together for a couple of months now. He's lovely, isn't he?'

'You and Richard are going out with each other?'

'Yes. Are you OK?'

'Mmm?'

How was I going to break the news to Eva? Her cancer hadn't nibbled at his psyche; it wasn't illness that had caused his desertion. It was another woman. What a guy. He had walked out on her and didn't have the balls to let her know. Would she care? Perhaps she already knew.

'Have you fallen asleep? Jake? I have to change here. It was nice meeting you. See you soon. 'Bye.'

Yasmin vanished into Hammersmith station, the train doors closed and I trundled underground.

It was obvious. It was just that I hadn't admitted it to myself: I was Eva's lover now. I had swapped places with Richard during the month I'd been away and transformed my life for ever. Was that any worse than him running off with a new girlfriend? Were we as faithless as each other? Was it coincidence that I'd picked up where he had left off to become his wife's lover? I'd have to wait until Eva got back next week to tell her. In the meantime I wanted home.

Home seemed strange. I was strange.

'Hi, Patrick?'

There was no reply. I dumped the case in my room and found a pile of mail, mostly in brown envelopes: the bank, the loan people and Barclaycard. It could wait. There was a letter from Charlotte Street clap clinic – I was clean. The place looked gloomy, and I guessed summer had gone while I was away. I checked the answerphone: it was on the verge of a nervous breakdown, ninety-three messages. Pedro and Max wanting to know where I was and why had I missed the doggy shower? A dozen me's, whoever they were. Lowlife Mark was obsessing. I had told him I was off, hadn't I? Bugger, a message from Visa: I must be in deep shit. There were any number of invitations to parties that had been and gone. A message from Giovanni: 'Jake, I don't know what happen to you. Maybe you stay on holiday. I'm going home now, back to Italy. Funny, eh? I'm following you back to Italy. I'll call you. *Ciao*, *ragazzo*.'

And one from Richard. 'Jake, hi, it's Richard here. I've had some sad news from Italy. Eva died last night. I'm sorry. Perhaps you might call me when you get this message.' Beep.

She'd done what? Replay. 'Jake, hi, it's Richard here. I've had some sad news from Italy. Eva died last night. I'm sorry. Perhaps you might call me when you get this message.' Beep.

Replay. 'Jake, hi, it's Richard here. I've had some sad news from Italy. Eva died last night. I'm sorry. Perhaps you might call me when you get this message.' Beep.

AFTERMATH

'Hi, Erin, I'm back.'

I'd made this call before. It was like the call I'd made when Louis died, but this time I was broken-hearted. My hand and the receiver were wet, so was my cheek – the voice was still bearing up, though.

'Jakey, you're home. I've missed you so much. When am I going to see you?'

'I'd like to see you now. Can you come over straight away? Eva's died.'

That was it. I'd said it. Same words, different person. I didn't have any insides to bawl out this time: I was drained and she was gone. I walked through the flat aimlessly picking up and putting down ornaments. I looked in the freezer: there was half a bottle of frozen vodka. I opened it and started to drink as I waited for Erin.

'She died at Maria's place while I was sleeping in Rome. It was only twenty-four hours ago, babes.'

'Jake, I'm so sorry.'

'I last saw Eva standing on the doorstep in Stromboli waving goodbye and then she turned back into the house . . .'

Erin put her arms around me and hugged me tight.

'She lied to me, babes. She wasn't coming home. She knew she was going to die, she knew we wouldn't be together. It was fantasy, wasn't it, Erin? Do you think it was mine or hers?'

'It's OK, Jake.'

'No, it's not. I love her.' A month of memory sprang out in my head. 'She said to me something like "Nothing stays as it should, we get it perfect and then it goes again." I know what she meant now.'

Eva had salvaged her little bit of heaven one last time. We'd built and sailed our boats. She was complete and I was daydreaming of a friend with a lump and long chiffon scarves.